WANTING HAPPILY EVER AFTER

ELENA AITKEN

Wanting Happily Ever After

Also by Elena Aitken

Ever After

Choosing Happily Ever After

Needing Happily Ever After

Wanting Happily Ever After

Fighting Happily Ever After

The McCormicks

Love in the Moment

Only for a Moment

One more Moment

In this Moment

From this Moment

Our Perfect Moment

Stand Alone Stories

All We Never Knew

Drawing Free

Sugar Crash

Composing Myself

Betty & Veronica

The Escape Collection

Vegas

Nothing Stays in Vegas

Return to Vegas

Goodbye Gifts

Tempting Gifts

Holiday Gifts

Promised Gifts

Accidental Gifts

The Castle Mountain Lodge Collection: Books 1-3

The Castle Mountain Lodge Collection: Books 4-6

The Castle Mountain Lodge Collection: Books 7-9

The Castle Mountain Lodge Complete Collection

Destination Paradise

Shelter by the Sea

Escape to the Sun

Hidden in the Sand - Available Soon!

Bears of Grizzly Ridge

His to Protect

His to Seduce

His to Claim

Hers to Take

His to Defend

His to Tame

His to Seek

Hers for the Season

Bears of Grizzly Ridge: Books 1-4

Bears of Grizzly Ridge: Books 5-8

Halfway Series

Halfway to Nowhere

Halfway in Between

Halfway to Christmas

Chapter One

IT WAS HOT. The kind of hot that made sitting on metal bleachers, shoulder to shoulder with dozens of other parents, a special kind of torture, especially when what you should be doing was sitting in the shade by the river with your feet in the water and a cold drink in your hand. But that wasn't an option for Sarah Lewis, not with her six-year-old daughter, Rory, running down the length of the soccer field, her teammates and friends next to her, long braids streaming behind her as she moved as fast as she could toward the goal.

For the life of her, Sarah could not imagine how any of them had so much energy on such a hot July afternoon, but none of the kids looked nearly as wilted as the parents. And if they could do it…she stood and cheered as loud as she could as Rory kicked the ball toward the net. There was no way the ball would go in. It was headed straight to the center of the goal… and the opposing team's goalie, who looked to be at least twice the size of the rest of the team. She'd easily be able to stop it. Sarah clutched her hands together and mentally prepared herself for Rory's disappointment.

The ball moved, almost in slow motion. The goalie made

her move. She opened her arms and jumped...right over the ball. Before anyone even realized what had happened, the ball was in the net and the referee blew the whistle, making it official.

Sarah exchanged glances with two of the other parents, Myrna and Jocelyn, on either side of her. The other mothers shook their heads in disbelief for a moment before leaping up and cheering. The team had just won! The Glacier Falls Grizzlies were going to play in the championship game!

Both the kids on the field and the parents and spectators in the stands erupted in cheers and screaming. Sarah watched as the realization of what had just happened hit her daughter. Rory's six-year-old face transformed. She dropped her hands momentarily to her knees. Her head dangled for a moment before she looked up, lifted her arms in the air, and let out a whoop of joy.

"She did it. She really did it." She shook her head and laughed at herself. After all, it was just a summer league child's soccer game, but she couldn't contain her excitement. It was a big deal to Rory, which meant it was a big deal to her.

"She did awesome!" Jocelyn wrapped her in a quick hug. "The girls played so well this season."

Sarah nodded and her gaze traveled across the field to where the team had met in a quick huddle to cheer their opposition and go shake hands. Her eyes landed on the coach, towering above his little players, a ball cap on his head to shield him from the sun, a matching red jersey, with "Coach" emblazoned on the back, right under "Birchwood," the name of the team's corporate sponsor—and the head coach's restaurant. Brody Morris held his ever-present clipboard in hand, and used it as a prop to wave in the air as the girls ran through their three cheers and went to shake hands with the other team. A fluttering sensation landed in her stomach when he turned toward her and raised his free hand in a small wave. A sensation that was happening more and more frequently lately. After all, he *was* very good-looking. Especially when he was playing the role of super coach.

"He's the best coach we've ever had," Myrna said, distracting her from staring at Brody.

"He really stepped up," someone else said.

"We're pretty lucky that you're dating Brody Morris, Sarah."

Her stomach fell, the flutterings squashed as Sarah whipped around to see who'd spoken. Audrey Hill smiled sweetly at Sarah, but there was nothing sweet intended by the comment, and they both knew it.

"We're not dating." Sarah hated that she even had to say something, particularly to Audrey. But if she didn't say anything, the rumors would start. And knowing Audrey, in less than twenty-four hours, the entire town would have heard that Sarah and Brody were not only a hot couple, but that they were expecting twins and moving in together, or something equally ludicrous. It didn't even matter if it wasn't based in truth; Audrey had a special gift of starting trouble. Trouble that, for whatever reason, she liked to aim in Sarah's direction.

It didn't help that Audrey's little girl, Clara, was Rory's favorite playmate.

"Well, you sure spend a lot of time together," Audrey continued, her voice carefully measured. "So if that's not dating, I don't know what is."

Sarah came up with a hundred different comebacks, but ultimately, shook her head and decided not to say anything. Audrey Hill wasn't worth it. Instead, she turned away, and looked straight at Byron Smith, single dad of Annie, one of Rory's teammates. He smiled kindly, as if to offer support, but Sarah couldn't help but think there was more behind his smile.

Byron had asked her out on more than one occasion and every time, Sarah had come up with an excuse. It wasn't that

Byron wasn't a nice man. He really was. But…it was always something. At first, it was because she just wasn't ready to date. And then, after a while…there was Brody. She hadn't lied to Audrey; they really weren't dating. They were friends. Best friends. And even if she did get that ridiculous fluttering feeling in her gut when he was around, it didn't matter because Brody would never be more than a friend. She valued him in her life too much for that. No way was she going to screw things up by dating. Even if she was open to that—which she wasn't.

She snuck a glance over to where Brody was gathering up the equipment on the sidelines and her stomach fluttered again.

No.

She wasn't going there. And definitely not with Brody.

Sarah knew she was her own worst enemy when it came to overthinking the situation, but she couldn't help it.

Thankfully, Rory saved her from any further thinking on the subject and chose that moment to holler up at her. "Mom! Did you see that, Mom?"

"I sure did, kiddo!" Without another look at anyone, Sarah gathered up her bag and made her way down the bleachers toward her daughter. She picked her up and squeezed her. "You were awesome. The game-winning goal! Wow."

"Wow indeed." Sarah's father, Ed Walker, appeared and Rory clambered into his arms. "Good job, Rory. I'm so proud of you."

"I didn't know you were here, Dad."

With a kiss on her head, Ed put his granddaughter down and she ran off to sit with her team in the shade of a tree to eat orange slices and celebrate their win. "I got here right after the second half started," he said. "Sorry I was late. I lost track of time in the garage."

Her dad had always been a putterer, with more projects than Sarah could keep straight. He still worked as Glacier Falls' fire chief, but more and more, Sarah could see that what he really wanted to focus on were his countless projects. And his granddaughter. Ed was a grade-A grandfather. He never missed an important date, but more importantly, he never missed anything Rory thought was important.

"Do you think she noticed I was late?" Ed looked with concern to the little girl, who didn't look as if she had a care in the world.

"You were here for the most important part and that's all that matters." She gave her dad a quick hug. "Thanks for coming. It means the world, Dad."

"You know I wouldn't miss it."

She did know. Still, it was worth saying, and she didn't like to miss an opportunity to tell her father how much she appreciated him.

After Sarah's mom died when she was barely a toddler, it had just been the two of them. And then, after the accident that had left Sarah a widow five years earlier, when Rory was only a baby, Sarah had leaned heavily on her father.

"Wasn't that a great game?" Brody, clipboard still in hand, appeared next to her. Sarah couldn't help but notice how he always made a point to greet her before any of the other parents. It was a detail that didn't seem to be lost on anyone, her father included. Next to her, Ed tensed ever so slightly. "What did you think of that, Mr. Walker? Pretty great game, wasn't it?"

"It was pretty close there until the end." Ed crossed his arms over his chest, but his lips twitched up into a flicker of smile before it disappeared again. "It's a good thing that granddaughter of mine is so quick."

She didn't know what it was, but it didn't seem to matter what Brody did or said; her father didn't seem to like him very much. She couldn't figure it out because Brody had been a great friend to her over the last few months. He'd been nothing but helpful and kind and...she forced herself to stop the line of thinking she was on as the fluttering in her stomach made a reappearance.

"That is a good thing, Mr. Walker," Brody answered diplomatically. "She's a very talented little girl." He turned to smile at Sarah. It was a simple action, but it warmed her. "I should go make my rounds," he said to her. "But I'll give you a call later. I have an ice cream cake in the freezer at the restaurant that needs to be tested, and I thought Rory might want to help out."

Sarah laughed. "Oh, I think she'd love to help you out with that."

"Sounds good." Brody put his hand on her arm and squeezed.

Did he hold it just a moment longer than was necessary? If Sarah had any experience with men at all, she might know. But beyond her late husband, she'd never even dated. She smiled as he took his leave and went to talk to the other parents, who were all waiting to congratulate their star coach.

She watched as he was swallowed up by them with cheers and pats on the back before turning back to her father. Ed's mouth was still turned down in a frown. She stopped herself before reminding her dad, just like everyone else, that she wasn't dating Brody. Because even though he hadn't said as much, Sarah was pretty sure that was her father's issue. Just as he'd remained single, it seemed that he thought his daughter should do the same. But he didn't have to worry—she had no intention of coupling up again. Like father, like daughter.

Suddenly exhausted and overwhelmed by the heat, she shook her head and ignored her dad and whatever it was that he clearly wanted to say. "I'm melting," she said instead. "Let's go celebrate Rory's goal with some iced tea."

Brody Morris tried to stay focused on the parents who were showering him with completely undeserved praise. After all, it was youth summer league soccer, not the World Cup. First place prize was a medal. The same as every other place. But to the parents of Glacier Falls, his adopted hometown, he might as well have been training their daughters for the Olympics.

"What do you think their odds of winning are, Coach?"

"That team from Cedar Springs is pretty tough."

"I heard they have a ringer."

"A ringer? Does anyone check the birth certificates of these kids?"

Brody handled each of the questions, with a smile and a chuckle. "Win or lose, you should all be so proud of your girls out there. They're playing their hearts out and having so much fun," he said good-naturedly. "They're all great kids. We should celebrate that."

"And their championship," Audrey Hill said confidently. "I mean, it's obvious that they're going to win. We should plan a party as a wrap-up."

Brody shook his head, but did his best not to look disagreeable. He'd met women like Audrey Hill before, and he knew well enough to stay on their good side. The last thing he wanted or needed was to be involved in any kind of drama, or to have Audrey Hill on his bad side, which would be worse. He tried to sneak a glance at Sarah, but she was turned away from him, kneeling on the grass, helping Rory unlace her cleats. Sarah had mentioned once or twice that Audrey had mastered the art of passive-aggressive bitchiness. Something about *mean girl* syndrome or something like that. Whatever it was, Brody believed her and did his best to keep Audrey at arm's length.

"A wind-up party sounds like a great idea." He smiled. "Let me know the details."

"Oh, I thought maybe Sarah could organize it." Her voice dripped with a false sweetness. "After all, she didn't bring team snacks as much as everyone else. It's really the least she could do."

Brody noticed a few of the other parents roll their eyes and shake their heads in disbelief, but not one of them said anything. He knew, just as well as they all knew, that Sarah did her best to attend all of the games and practices. But there were a few times when she wasn't able to make it due to work because she was a single mom who essentially supported and raised her little girl by herself. Obviously that little detail wasn't about to be recognized by this group.

He usually bit his tongue, in an effort to remain a neutral party as much as possible, but this was too much. "You know Sarah does her best to be here whenever she can. She has a lot on her plate."

Audrey took a step back and raised her eyebrow. "Sounds like someone is getting a little defensive." She clucked her tongue. "I didn't mean to stir up anything."

That's *exactly* what she'd meant. Still, Brody kept a smile on his face. "Oh, of course, Audrey. All I'm saying is that Sarah—"

"Makes sure that her father brings the team snacks when she can't be here. And has never missed once."

Brody turned to see Sarah, speaking about herself in the third person, walk up to the group. He tried, but failed, to stifle a smile.

"And I'm pretty sure you know, Audrey, that my father brings Rory's snacks on *all* the days that I get caught up at work. After all, the snacks are assigned by *child* and not by *parent.* Isn't that right?"

Audrey stammered and struggled over her words, but finally swallowed hard and nodded curtly. "I was just—"

"Oh, I know what you were doing," Sarah continued, a sweet smile on her face. Only her crossed arms over her chest gave away her true feelings about the woman.

Brody couldn't help but be impressed by her self-restraint.

"And yes, if you're unable to host the wind-up party, by all means, I'd be more than happy to take it off your plate."

"Oh, that's not…I wasn't saying that—"

"No, no," Sarah continued. "I don't mind at all. I know how busy you are with…" She tilted her head and innocently asked, "What is it that keeps you so busy?"

Brody couldn't help it; a chuckle slipped out of his mouth. He tried to cover it with a cough, but he couldn't be sure it worked. Not that anyone paid him any attention. All eyes were on Audrey.

"Well." The other woman pulled herself up and pushed her shoulders back. "I don't think—"

"Don't worry about a thing." Sarah waved her hand casually. "I'll take care of all the details." She beamed at the other parents, who were all watching the little drama unfold. "I'll sort out some details on my end and send out an email. Have a great day, everyone." And just like that, she spun on her heel and, with her head held high, walked away.

Like all of the others, Brody watched her go with sheer amazement on his face. He couldn't help but notice the way Byron Smith was watching Sarah particularly closely. Brody forced himself not to let it bother him. Of course there'd be men interested in her. After all, she was an amazing woman. Strong, hardworking, and gorgeous—even though she clearly had no idea how good-looking she was. He'd been spending more and more time with Sarah since moving to Glacier Falls, and he was really enjoying getting to know her.

He'd been attracted to her instantly, but it didn't take long to learn that she was a dedicated single mom whose entire life was devoted to her little girl. It hadn't put Brody off, though; it had only made him more cautious. Maybe too cautious, because he'd clearly been friend-zoned. Hell, from what he could tell, every man had been friend-zoned. Sarah didn't seem the least bit interested in dating. But at least he had her as his closest friend. And that was something. But as much as Brody did know about Sarah, she still had a few surprises up her sleeve. And dealing with mean moms was an impressive skill, to say the least.

He made small talk for a few more minutes, gave high fives to all the kids and took his own leave shortly after.

It was hot, and he would have loved to spend the rest of the day sitting in the shade somewhere, preferably with his feet in the water, underneath the cool branches of a pine tree in the forest, but it was not to be. He had a restaurant to run, and despite his wildest dreams, Birchwood wasn't yet running itself.

The moment he stepped inside the restaurant, he knew something was wrong. If it was hot outside, it was an absolute sauna inside the walls. He went immediately to the thermostat on the wall, and groaned. He tapped at it, the extent of his knowledge of how to make it work again.

"Shit."

The last thing he needed was one more thing that wasn't working. Not when his list was already growing beyond the scope of things he would be able to handle—or afford. But air conditioning was going to have to go on the list. When he moved to Glacier Falls from his small town in rural Saskatchewan, he never would have expected it to get so hot in the middle of the summer. After all, wasn't it supposed to be cool in the middle of the mountains? Apparently not so much. Not that he minded. At least, he wouldn't have minded the heat if the air conditioning wasn't broken.

How was he supposed to serve customers when it was so hot?

He pushed his way into the kitchen, where it must have been at least ten degrees warmer, if it were even possible.

"Tell me you brought a repair guy?" Amy, his head chef,

greeted him from behind the stove. "I feel like I'm going to pass out."

"How long has it been broken?" Forgoing his usual chef jacket, Brody grabbed an apron and tied it around his waist. "This is crazy."

"You're telling me." Amy wiped her brow and leaned against the counter. "I was going to get some stock started, but I think I might just abandon that plan altogether."

"Agreed. Try not to use the stove or the oven for anything. Maybe we can offer a special cool summer menu?" His brain started to spin with ideas as he spoke. "We can do a gazpacho, and salads, of course. Maybe a ceviche and some sushi rolls."

"I like it." Amy switched off the stove and her attempt at stock. "Especially if it keeps me even a little bit cool."

"And for dessert, I'll whip up some sorbets and maybe another ice cream cake."

"*Another* ice cream cake?" Amy wiggled her eyebrows.

Brody had hired her about three months ago, and they'd become quick friends. She was a few years younger than he was, fresh out of a basic culinary program in the city and she'd proved to be not only a lot of fun to spend his days with, but also an incredibly talented chef. It was only a matter of time before he lost her to bigger and better things. He would miss her on a professional level and as a close friend when that day came.

"Don't think I didn't notice that cake in the freezer," she continued. "I also noticed the note on it that said not to touch."

"It was a test cake."

"Riiigght." Amy rolled her eyes. "A *test* cake. Interesting that it also happens to be mint chocolate chip."

"Why is that interesting?"

"Oh, only because I happen to know that mint chocolate chip is a certain little girl's favorite flavor."

Brody turned to look at his friend. "And how do you know that's Rory's favorite flavor?"

"It's every little girl's favorite flavor, isn't it?"

She shot him a look, but Brody wasn't imagining the blush he saw on his friend's face. Sarah had mentioned more than once that Amy had been spending quite a bit of time around Rory's auntie, Nicole. Brody definitely wasn't going to ask, because it wasn't his business, but judging by Amy's reaction, his suspicions were correct and there was something more than friendship going on between the two.

"Sure it is." He winked. "But you're right. It is Rory's favorite, and I was going to take it over there later. But first, let me pull together some type of hot weather menu." He moved to leave Amy in the kitchen, to head into his tiny office, when she stopped him.

"Don't forget to call a repair man."

He flinched, hoping she couldn't see his reaction. "Of course. I'll find time to call a repair man." He dropped his head and rubbed his temple as he mentally added, *And the money to pay for it.*

Chapter Two

SARAH ADJUSTED the fan in Rory's room so it wasn't aimed directly at the little girl, but just over her sleeping body. It was futile, really, to try to get any real air movement in the house when it was so hot outside, but if it meant that Rory wouldn't wake up sweating and uncomfortable, she'd give it a shot. Before she left, she picked up the stuffed bunny from the floor and tucked it under Rory's arm, dropped a kiss on her forehead, and slowly crept out of the room, leaving her daughter to sleep.

"Investing in an air conditioner seems like a really good use of funds right now," she moaned as she made her way outside and onto the back deck, where Brody was lounging on the wicker furniture she'd invested in last year. There was a slight evening breeze, and with the sun finally starting to set in the summer sky, it should be starting to cool off a little. Hopefully. She flopped down next to him on the lounger.

"I didn't think people got air conditioning in the mountains." Brody grinned. "At least not in their homes. It turns out they're more or less required in restaurants." He shook his head a little and pinched the bridge of his nose.

He'd shown up at her house after the dinner rush at Birchwood, an ice cream cake in his hands, and stress lines on his handsome face. He hadn't wanted to talk about it, just said something about it being crazy at the restaurant, and she'd let it go. They'd each eaten a slice of mint chocolate chip ice cream cake. It was Rory's favorite flavor, and despite Sarah's reservations about giving her ice cream so late in the evening, there was no way she could refuse. Rory loved Brody, and as they'd both pointed out, it was a celebration. After all, they'd made it to the play-offs.

Besides, it *was* summer. And in the end, Rory had gone to sleep easily, completely unaffected by the ice cream.

"I have definitely thought about it," Sarah said, returning to the conversation of air conditioning. "But really, it only gets this hot for a few weeks out of the year. I can struggle through. What were you saying about Birchwood? Is the A/C down again?"

"Again?" He tilted his head. "Has Amy been talking?"

Sarah shrugged. "She mentioned it to Nicole, who—"

"Mentioned it to you." He shook his head. "I hope it doesn't get around," he said. "No one in town is going to want to eat in a sauna, and my patio space is only so big. Summer menu or not."

A flash of guilt went through her as she remembered the conversation with her sister-in-law. "I'm sure Nicole only mentioned it to me because she knows that you and I are... friends," she finished lamely. She watched his face for any indication that it could ever be anything more than friends, but his face didn't change. She'd been thinking more and more about trying to date again, and ironically, it was her sister-in-law who'd become more and more interested in Sarah's love life, pushing her to get out there. But that didn't mean it had to be Brody who she went out with.

"And I mean," she recovered and spoke quickly to cover up

any awkwardness, "Amy would have only told Nicole because they are…" She gave up and shook her head. "I mean, I don't know. I assume they're dating." Her sister-in-law came out to her family when she was in high school, but beyond a few short relationships when she lived in the city, Nicole's love life had been almost as nonexistent as her own. She chuckled a little as she reached forward to grab a glass of water. Changing her mind, she reached instead for the cooler that held a few bottles of beer.

She held one up to Brody, who nodded.

"Absolutely."

Sarah twisted off her cap and held out her bottle for a cheers.

"I knew there was something going on there," Brody said with a laugh. "I mean, I wasn't going to ask Amy or anything, but she sure talks about Nicole a lot."

Sarah grinned. Her late husband's older sister was a huge part of her and Rory's life, and one of Sarah's best friends. Nicole had confided in her many times that she was interested in the chef. And although there still didn't seem to be an official label on anything, if the glow in her sister-in-law's cheeks was any indication, she was absolutely smitten.

Despite herself, Sarah couldn't help but feel a little jealous of Nicole. It had been so long since she'd felt the excitement of a new relationship. And she'd been barely older than seventeen the one and only time she'd ever felt it. She'd started dating Josh in high school and he'd been her only boyfriend. Married shortly after they graduated, and then pregnant during nursing school, there'd never been an opportunity for any actual dating. And if she were honest with herself, she wasn't sure she'd ever actually had the whole butterflies and excitement with Josh that everyone talked about. It had just been…comfortable.

She shook her head to keep from going down that path. There was no point. "It's nice, but…"

"But what?"

"This is going to sound so bad." Sarah swallowed hard and for a moment debated on saying anything at all. Maybe it was the little bit of beer she had, or the heat, but she made the decision just to say what was on her mind. "I'm kind of jealous."

"Jealous?" Brody sat up and raised his eyebrow. "Of Nicole? I didn't think Amy was really your type."

Sarah burst out laughing. "She's not."

Brody shook his head and ran a hand through his hair. "Then what?" he asked. "What are you jealous of Nicole for?"

Sarah's laughter stopped suddenly. "That feeling."

Brody tipped his head in question but didn't speak, so Sarah continued. "You know," she said. "That new dating feeling. The excitement, the butterflies…the anticipation of what's coming next. All of it. It's been a long time since I felt that way." She dropped her head back and looked up to the evening sky. "A *long* time."

Brody didn't say anything right away, and as the silence grew, she started to think that maybe she should have kept her mouth shut. Her cheeks burned with embarrassment.

Finally, she took a breath and swallowed hard. "I don't actually know why I said that."

"Why?"

She shook her head. "Because I actually don't think I am jealous. It all sounds so…overwhelming."

"I don't know." He didn't look at her as he spoke, but instead tipped his head up to the sky. "It doesn't have to be. It can be amazing."

"Then why aren't you doing it?" The second she asked the question, she regretted it. Sarah loved spending time with Brody. She'd come to depend on him, in a way. That would all change if he started dating someone. Which was probably why in all the time they'd hung out and been getting to know each other, she'd never asked him why he was single. After all, he was a good man, successful, incredibly good-looking. No doubt half the single ladies in town, never mind the tourists, would be interested in him. But it was in her best—and totally selfish—interests for him to stay single. The idea of him dating someone just didn't feel right. She just couldn't picture it.

He didn't answer right away but right when Sarah was going to change the subject to something safer, he looked at her. "It's just not been the right time."

She nodded. That made sense. He'd been pretty busy getting Birchwood up and running, and then with coaching the soccer team, he probably didn't have a lot of extra time anyway.

"Why don't you give it a try, Sarah? I mean, it's been…how long?"

She swallowed hard against the lump in her throat. It didn't matter how long it had been. It didn't get any easier. "Five. Almost six years."

Sarah appreciated that he didn't tell her she was being ridiculous by waiting so long to get back into the dating world the way most people did when they found out she'd been a widow for so long.

Instead, he nodded. "And you haven't considered getting back out there?"

She shrugged.

They sat in silence for a few minutes, each sipping at their drinks before Brody spoke again. "It was an accident, right?"

Sarah hesitated, but eventually nodded. It was an accident. That was the official report. A drowning. An accident. A terrible, tragic accident. That was what the investigation had ruled.

She'd never spoken it out loud, but that didn't stop her from questioning it. *Had they gotten it wrong?*

"I heard he saved a child from drowning." Brody added, "That's pretty amazing."

"Right." She looked down. The familiar guilt filled her. "The details got a little messed up," she finally said. "There wasn't a child, but some people heard that and there was a newspaper story that ran it and...well, they printed a retraction but even so...anyway...I never bothered to correct anyone."

She'd never really told anyone that part of things before. Not unless they asked. Which most didn't. It had always just been easier for everyone to believe Josh had been a hero.

Brody nodded in understanding. "I could see that."

"Really?"

"Absolutely. I can't even imagine what that time would have been like for you."

They sat in silence for a moment before Brody spoke again.

"And he was the love of your life?" He took a sip of his beer. "Is that why you haven't been able to date again?"

It was what most people assumed and over the years, Sarah had found it easier just to let people think what they wanted. It offered them an easy explanation for why she chose to stay single. It sure was a hell of a lot easier than the alternative.

She looked over at Brody and contemplated telling him the truth. But ultimately she just shrugged. "Maybe I will start dating."

It was a throw-away comment, but Brody sat upright and stared directly at her, a grin on his face.

"Really? You will?"

She shrugged again. "Byron Smith has asked me out a few times. Maybe I'll—"

"You're going to go out with Byron Smith? Annie's dad?" Brody raised his eyebrow and almost laughed.

Something about his response pissed her off a little. *Wasn't she good enough for Byron?* She sat up straighter. "Why not?"

Brody outright laughed, only causing Sarah to bristle further.

"Why not, Brody?" She leaned forward and stared at him.

"Why shouldn't I go out with Byron? What's wrong with him?" She truly had no real intention to go out with him, but Brody's reaction was rapidly changing her mind. "He's a nice guy."

"That's just it." Brody laughed harder, and shook his head. "He's a *nice* guy. A banker, single dad. Nice and solid. Super dependable."

Sarah fumed. Byron *was* a nice guy. And she was a nice woman. And if she wanted to date him, she would. And she would not let Brody make her feel any way at all about it. Her annoyance rose, which was likely what led her to say what she did. "Well, I'm going out with him." The words came out of her mouth before she even realized what she'd said. "So I guess I'll see for myself if he's a nice guy or not."

In a flash, Brody was silent. He paused, his beer bottle halfway to his mouth. "Wait? Seriously? You're actually going out with him?"

It didn't seem so funny all of a sudden, but still, Sarah nodded. "I am. Later this week." She took a deep pull on her beer bottle. She'd sort out the logistical details of the *actual* date later.

"Really? Next week?" Brody hoped he sounded casual and unaffected. After all, he didn't have any right to sound anything but. They were, in fact, only friends. Still.

What. The. Actual. Fuck?

"Yup." She nodded and took another sip of her beer. "Like I said, he's asked me out a few times, but there's no time like the present, right?"

He nodded, because what else was he going to do? "Why not?"

"Exactly." She looked directly at him. "Why not?"

This was his chance. This was where he could tell her exactly why not. This was his moment. Where he could tell her that he'd wanted to ask her on a proper date from the moment he'd met her. But he'd waited. He'd given her time. He'd...damn it.

"Well, that'll be *nice*." He knew he was being a dick, but he couldn't help it. "Byron is a very *nice* man and I'm sure you'll have a perfectly *nice time.*" *Not at all like the amazing, life-altering time you'd have with me on a date.* He wanted to say it, but he couldn't. It wasn't fair. Not now.

"It will be."

If Sarah thought he was being a jerk, she didn't say it. But he was being a jerk and he couldn't seem to stop himself. "I mean, if you like that kind of thing."

She raised an eyebrow.

"You know," he continued. "Safe, predictable, mundane."

"Mundane?"

Brody regretted his choice of words. He was being a first-class asshole. There was nothing wrong with Byron. He'd meant it when he'd said he was nice. That was the only way to describe it. He was *nice.* He was a good dad. Annie was a good kid. He had a good, stable job at the bank, an amicable relationship—from all accounts—with his ex-wife, and he was...*mundane.*

"I'm sorry," Brody said quickly. "I shouldn't have said that. Byron is a good guy and I'm proud of you for getting back out there. Really."

She nodded and looked out into the dark yard.

He couldn't help but think of the ring in the top drawer of his dresser. It was his grandmother's ring. A ruby set in platinum. It wasn't an engagement ring by any stretch of the imagination, not at all, and even if it was, he wasn't so delusional to think that he was ever going to give it to Sarah. But yet...when he'd opened the package his mother had sent him from home with a variety of items, including the ring, the only finger he could picture it on was Sarah's. It was inexplicable, considering they were nothing more than friends. But still.

He blushed and inwardly groaned when he'd remembered how he'd shown the ring to their mutual friend, Faith Turner. They'd all been at a wedding reception to celebrate Damon Banks and Katie Langdon's nuptials. He'd catered it, of course, and although he'd never usually drink on the job, it was a friend's event, and not so entirely professional. So he'd had a few drinks, which had likely made him a little sentimental, and perhaps, wishful.

Brody had been watching Sarah and Rory twirling on the dance floor when he'd shown Faith the ring that had only just arrived. He'd told her that he was going to give it to Sarah.

He could just die of embarrassment now. Hell, he couldn't even ask Sarah on a date. And clearly, she wasn't interested in him beyond a friendship. He'd jumped the gun, that was all. He shook his head and took a deep pull on his beer bottle, draining it.

When he put it down, Sarah was watching him. "What?"

"I was just wondering what you were thinking." She tilted her head and her dark hair fell down over her shoulder.

She was gorgeous, and she didn't even realize it. Even at the end of a long day, her effortless beauty took his breath away. Brody resisted the urge to tuck her hair behind her ear so he could see her big brown eyes better.

When he didn't answer right away, she asked again, "Well? What are you thinking?"

He almost laughed out loud. There was no way he was telling her what was going on in his head. No way. Especially considering he'd been so clearly friend-zoned. Instead, he shrugged and reached for another beer. "I was just wondering if you needed a babysitter for your date?"

Sarah's eyes squeezed shut for a moment and when she

reopened them, she looked as if she were going to tell him something. Her mouth opened and closed.

"Because I wouldn't want anything to stop you from going out with Byron Smith." He couldn't even believe he was still talking. He should be telling her not to go out with him, not making it easier for her. He needed to step up. But he'd never been good at the whole dating thing, especially not when he really liked someone, and he *really liked* Sarah. He thought he'd been doing the right thing by moving slow, not pressuring her into going out with him, being her friend. Her *best* friend. But what he really should be doing was telling her that Byron was absolutely not the right guy for her, because *he* was. He was just about to retract his offer when Sarah beat him to it.

"That would be great, thanks. I'll let you know the details, okay?"

Brody nodded and silently chastised himself. There was no way he was going to wreck her date just because he was an idiot. That wasn't fair. So, he bit his tongue. "You know what else you need some details for?" He looked at her and wiggled his eyebrows until she groaned in understanding.

"The stupid wind-up party." Sarah dropped her head back on the lounger. "Why did I open my big mouth on that one?"

The conversation shifted and just like that, the strange tension between them was gone and they were back to the easy familiarity that they usually enjoyed together. "You opened your mouth because she was being a bitch."

"It's true," Sarah agreed. "But I probably should have let her. Because now I have to organize the wind-up party in two weeks, and I bet it's only a matter of days before I get a text message, if I don't have one already, with all of her *ideas*." She reached for her cell phone. "And…" She tapped at her phone before holding it up. "She's already texted."

"Seriously?" He really didn't understand women. Still, he tried not to laugh. "Won't she just be glad she's not doing it?"

Sarah laughed. "Oh, hell no. Instead, she'll passive-aggressively offer me 'help' in the form of all her ideas and when I don't take them, she'll criticize every little thing at the party."

Brody shook his head. "It's a soccer wind-up party for six- and seven-year-olds."

"You think that matters?"

Sarah sat up and stared at him until he finally shook his head. *Apparently it didn't.*

"I have a feeling I'm going to regret this question," he said after a minute. "But do you need advice?" Brody reached for a fresh bottle of beer, crossed his legs, and leaned back.

Sarah stared at him dumbly. "I know how to throw a party, Brody."

"I'm sure you do." He tipped the bottle back and let the cold liquid cool him a little. "So tell her you don't need help."

"Right."

"Why not?"

"You can't just tell the Audrey Hills of the world that you don't need their help. That's like a challenge."

Brody blinked, unable to see her point. "And?" he finally asked. "What's wrong with that?"

"You've clearly not dealt with an Audrey Hill before."

"Clearly." He tried not to smile, because Sarah looked so serious as she stared at her phone. Obviously this Audrey got Sarah worked up. That was easy to see. And after talking to the other woman for more than a few minutes, he could understand why she might be aggravating, but for the life of him, he couldn't see why it was worth giving her the satisfaction.

"I've been dealing with not only the Audreys of the world, but *this* particular Audrey since the Baby and Me group when the girls were first born. She's..." Sarah shook her head. "Well, she seems to take a special pleasure from being better than me at...well, at pretty much everything."

"Why does that bother you, though? I don't get it." Brody

sat up. He genuinely didn't. As far as he was concerned, Audrey—with her perfectly applied makeup and styled hair without ever a strand out of place—didn't even come close to Sarah's genuine beauty. Her dark hair was almost always tied back in a ponytail; her T-shirts and cut-offs, when she wasn't at work, fit her just right and showed off all her curves. And her natural beauty didn't need any makeup. In fact, Brody liked her natural blush when he winked at her, better than any shade of makeup. And that was just their appearances. On the inside, there was no contest between the two women. Audrey, although he was sure she wasn't a bad woman, didn't have the genuine warmth that Sarah did. Something about Sarah made you want to be around her. Even if Brody hadn't been ridiculously attracted to her, he knew he wouldn't be able to stay away from her. She pulled people in.

But just because Brody didn't get it, didn't mean that there wasn't a real feeling there. And it was obvious that Sarah *was* bothered by her.

She sighed and dropped her head for a minute. "Honestly?"

He nodded.

"I don't really know. I think that because it's just me, I should be everything and be able to do everything. Like supermom. It's a pressure I've felt inside and then, when Audrey's around, there's an external pressure, too. Like I need to prove to the world that I *can* do it all." She shrugged. "It probably sounds stupid."

"It doesn't sound stupid. It sounds to me like a woman who's been on her own for too long, left to do it all. You don't need to prove anything to anyone. You're a fabulous mother. The best I know." Her lips twitched up into a small smile. He had to hold himself back from reaching out to her, just the same way he'd held himself back for months. "If it's important to you to prove to the Audrey Hills of the world that you can throw a kick-ass soccer wind-up party, let's do it."

She blinked her big brown eyes at him and shook her head a little. "*Let's*? As in, you and I? You want to help?"

He nodded. "Absolutely. I'm totally willing to help."

Especially if it meant spending more time with her. That's all he needed—just a bit more time to convince her that it was him who she wanted to go out with.

Chapter Three

FAITH TURNER TOOK up an entire corner table in Sweetie Pies, her papers, notebooks, and photographs from a recent photo shoot spread out in front of her. Her eyes continued to drift to one photo in particular. It was a shot of her friend Katie in her wedding dress by the river. Her back was turned to the camera, which was a good thing because Faith knew that her friend's eyes were sad when the picture was taken because she thought that her relationship with now-husband, Damon, was falling apart. What she didn't realize was that a few minutes later she'd be surprised with a huge wedding celebration and a declaration of love that even Faith, who steadfastly didn't believe in love, might have been swayed by.

It was one of Faith's favorite pictures and it would be perfect for the ad campaign she was planning for Ever After Ranch, her twin sister's—and now hers as well—wedding venue business. But it wasn't enough yet. She needed more pictures.

She laughed a little at herself at the idea that she was actually a co-owner of a wedding business of all things. Her laughter attracted the attention of other customers, but Faith didn't care. She smiled and even waved at one particularly nosy-looking older woman who didn't look very impressed with the display of mirth. Faith resisted sticking her tongue out at the woman and fortunately, her phone rang, distracting her further.

She glanced at the caller ID, smiled, and answered the call. "Hey, sis. On your way home yet?"

Faith could almost see her twin sister, Hope, rolling her eyes on the other end of the line, even as far away as Europe, where she was currently on an elaborate honeymoon with her new husband, Levi. "You know I'm not."

"You should be." Faith's smile fell a little. As much as she genuinely wanted her sister to be enjoying herself on her once-in-a-lifetime trip, she also wanted her home. A few weeks ago, that desire was out of selfish want so Hope could once again resume the operations of Ever After, which was, after all, her business baby. But now, the want to have Hope get on a plane and get back to Glacier Falls was all about having her sister home safe and sound, where she could make sure she was healthy.

Hope had been diagnosed with uterine cancer right before her wedding to her childhood sweetheart, Levi. They decided to take an elaborate trip around the world as they tried for a baby, and held off on Hope's *life-saving* surgery. And sure, they had her doctor's blessing, but it wasn't enough reassurance for a very worried sister. And now, with Hope's latest news, that they were in fact already pregnant, more than ever, Faith wanted her only family member back, safe and sound.

She also knew it was unlikely that her sister, stubborn as she was, was going to do anything before she was good and ready.

"We're in Ireland now," Hope continued, as if Faith hadn't spoken. "And before you ask, *yes*, I'm feeling great and *no*, I haven't had any Guinness. I'm leaving the drinking up to Levi for the time being."

Faith rolled her eyes, but couldn't help but smile.

"I promise, Faith," Hope said more seriously. "I'm fine. I feel fine and I've been in touch with my doctor back home. She's given me permission to stay. We're good."

"Okay," Faith said begrudgingly. "I know you're not going to take any stupid risks." *Especially not now that she was pregnant,* she thought but didn't bother saying out loud. It helped that Levi was there to take good care of her, and Faith knew the man loved her sister more than anything else in the world. He wouldn't let anything happen to her. "Tell me about Ireland."

For the next few minutes, Hope filled her in on all the sights they were seeing, the pubs Levi was enjoying, and the challenges of driving on the wrong side of the road in an impossibly tiny car on even more impossibly tiny streets.

When she was finished, Faith filled her sister in on the upcoming weddings they had on the books, including one more that Faith had booked all on her own. Most of the events had been set up before Hope had gone out of town, leaving some empty spaces in the calendar that Faith was starting to fill.

"I'm impressed, Faith. It sounds like you might actually be enjoying this wedding business after all."

"Don't get carried away. I'm doing you a favor. That's it." She glanced down at the papers and photos in front of her with all the details of the social media advertising campaign she was planning, but decided not to say anything. If it worked out, it would be a surprise for Hope. And if it didn't…then she wouldn't have to say anything at all.

"And Logan's helping you out?"

Much to her annoyance, Faith's stomach did an obnoxious little flip at the mention of the man. Even more annoying was that Hope asked. "You know he is." She sighed. "After all, you and Levi both asked him to." Before they'd left on their trip, the couple had asked Levi's cousin, Logan, to help her out with anything she needed. Which would have been fine—if what she needed was an overly confident, arrogant, extremely gorgeous, pain in the ass.

Whom she also happened to be annoyingly attracted to.

"What aren't you telling me, Faith?"

Her sister had the extra obnoxious twin sister trait of always knowing when Faith was holding back information—which, in this case, was that in a moment of weakness, she had let down her guard and given in to that annoying attraction when she kissed Logan. "Nothing," she lied. Half a world away, her sister didn't need to know anything. Especially considering Faith didn't know herself what it meant.

The bells over the door of the bakery jingled and Faith turned to see Nick walk in. She didn't know him well; in fact, she'd only met him a few times, once being at the surprise wedding celebration for Katie Langdon and her new husband Damon Banks the week before. But he was tall, dark, and fun to flirt with. And he was smiling right at her.

"I've gotta go," Faith said to her sister. "I have some things to take care of and there's someone I need to talk to."

After a quick good-bye, Faith put her phone down right as Nick, a coffee and plate in his hand, approached her table. "May I join you? I seem to have two of these delicious-looking scones."

"I never could say no to a fresh scone."

"Or some scintillating conversation with a handsome stranger?"

She burst out laughing. "Right, or that." He took the seat across from her while Faith piled up some of her scattered papers. "So you decided to stay in town for a bit?" She picked one of the scones off the table and broke off a piece.

"I did." Nick crossed one leg over the other and leaned back in his chair. "There seemed to be a few compelling reasons for me to stay."

"And what are those?"

29

He pretended to think for a moment before looking at her. "The mountains...Damon tells me the mountain biking is pretty great. These scones are pretty delicious..." He held it up. "And the people seem pretty all right."

She laughed and shook her head. "The scones *are* delicious. And the mountain biking is pretty fun, if you're into that type of thing."

"And the people?"

She took her time answering, enjoying the casual banter. Finally, she looked at him and grinned. "Oh, I think some of the people are pretty okay."

"Some?"

"Some more than others, for sure."

"Maybe some of those people might be interested in going on a date?"

The bells over the door jingled again as someone new entered. Faith didn't have to look to see who it was, because within seconds, the energy in the room shifted. The hairs on the back of Faith's neck stood up and a heat bloomed low in her belly. Slowly she turned, and confirmed her suspicions. Logan.

When had his mere presence started to affect her so dramatically?

He was staring directly at her, and their eyes connected. In an instant, the heat in her belly rushed throughout her body, flushing her face. Faith snapped her eyes shut and spun around.

"Are you okay?" Nick's voice was laced with concern and confusion.

She nodded and reached for her coffee. Not surprisingly, the hot liquid did nothing to ease her flush. But it did give her a moment to pull herself together and regain her composure. She was acting like a ridiculous schoolgirl. She didn't have feelings for Logan. Hell, she didn't *ever* have feelings for a man. She'd always prided herself on being and staying single.

Period.

So why was her heart racing?

"Faith?"

Nick was still staring at her. "I'm fine. Sorry." She smiled and forced her attention on the attractive friendly man in front of her instead of the attractive antagonistic one at the counter behind her. But as hard as she tried to focus on Nick, her entire body was annoyingly tuned in to Logan.

Faith took a breath and refocused on the man in front of her. "What were you saying?"

He chuckled and leaned back a little. "Are you sure you're okay?"

"Of course." It was clearly a lie, but to his credit, Nick didn't mention it.

"I was just asking if maybe you'd like to go out on—"

"Hi, Faith."

She spun, the question on Nick's lips forgotten when Logan approached.

It annoyed her to no end that she was so affected by this man, who had done nothing but drive her crazy for most of her life, particularly the last few months. But try as she might, she couldn't seem to do a damn thing about it.

"I'm not interrupting anything, am I?" Without waiting for an answer, Logan pulled up a seat and stared directly at her as he sipped at his coffee.

Faith did her best to ignore him, but judging by Nick's chuckle and the shake of his head, she wasn't having much success.

Chapter Four

BY MONDAY AFTERNOON, the weather still hadn't cooled. If anything, it was only getting hotter. Sarah couldn't remember the last time they'd had such a hot July. As she left Doctor Friesen's office, where she worked full-time as a nurse, the heat hit her like a wall. It was bearable while she was in the air conditioning, but being outside was a different story altogether. She was going to have to find a way to cool off. Ten minutes later, as she arrived on her sister-in-law's porch to pick up Rory, she was pretty sure she was going to melt completely.

"It's so insanely hot," she said when Nicole joined her on the porch. "This is unbearable."

"I agree." Nicole wore jean cut-offs and a tank top. Her thick blonde hair was piled up onto the top of her head, and with a glass of iced tea in her hand, she looked as if she weren't having any trouble at all staying cool. She offered Sarah the glass, which she took and drank readily.

"I was just telling Rory that we should all go to the lake this weekend to—"

"The lake?" Sarah almost spat out the iced tea as she choked on the word. "The lake?"

Nicole gave her a look that made it clear she was worried about Sarah's sanity. "Yes, the lake. Where else can we go to cool off?"

"You mentioned it to Rory?"

"Yup." Nicole nodded slowly. "Because it's like a million degrees out."

Sarah shook her head and turned away. *No. She did not mention the lake to Rory. No.*

"Sarah? Are you okay? What the—"

"No." Sarah spun around. "I am *not* okay. The lake, Nicole? *The lake?*"

Nicole glanced behind her into the house before stepping all the way out onto the porch. She shut the door behind her and gestured for Sarah to sit on the step. "I'm going to ask you something," she said, slowly and softly. "Even though I think I already know the answer."

Sarah nodded.

"Have you ever been back to the lake?"

She didn't bother answering; they both knew the answer. How could she go back to the lake that Josh drowned in? How could she ever sit on the beach and look at the once-innocent waves gently lapping at the shore and relive what had gone down that day?

She couldn't.

"Sarah, it's just a lake. It's okay."

She sat heavily on the step next to Nicole. "You've been back?"

She hesitated for a moment, but then Nicole nodded. "A few years ago," she said softly. "I'm not going to lie. It wasn't easy at first, but then I had to remember…what happened was a terrible accident, Sarah. And Josh loved the lake. He loved to swim. He wouldn't want me to stop going there. And I know he wouldn't want you and Rory to stop going there either."

He loved to swim.

Nicole's words reverberated in Sarah's head. Josh had loved to swim. And he was a strong swimmer, too. Which was why it had been such a shock when he'd drowned. The official report had been that he'd swum too far out and probably got tired or a cramp and couldn't make it back. But Sarah couldn't help but question it, and she knew Nicole would too if she knew the truth about that day and what had sent Josh into the lake for a swim in the first place. Which was why she could never tell her sister-in-law the truth. She'd never tell anyone. It was also why she'd let everyone believe the mistaken report that he'd been trying to save a child from drowning. It was wrong, yes.

But Josh was gone. The truth wouldn't bring him back and ultimately, it was less painful for everyone—except her—to assume it had been a terrible accident and not intentional. Especially because there was no way to know for sure.

"I don't know if I can do it," Sarah said slowly. "I don't know if I can take Rory there. Not after…"

Nicole put her hand on her leg. "You can. And you should."

Nicole smiled so kindly that something inside Sarah gave way. *Maybe it wouldn't be so bad. Maybe going back to the lake would be okay.*

"In fact," Nicole continued. "We should all go. Maybe get a big group together and make a day of it. That way, it might be less intense for you."

Sarah nodded and to her surprise, she liked that idea. Besides, Rory would like it. It could be fun. "Okay," she heard herself say.

"Really?"

Sarah nodded again before she could change her mind. A smile crossed her face. "Yes. Let's do it."

Nicole jumped up. "Awesome! It will be fun. I'll ask Amy if she wants to come and you bring Brody."

Sarah hesitated and turned to look up at Nicole. "Why would you say it like that?"

"What?"

Sarah stood. "Well, you just said that you'd bring Amy, because the two of you are seeing each other, and then you mentioned Brody the same way. Why?"

Nicole shook her head and laughed. "It's okay, Sarah. Really, you don't have to be scared to tell me."

"Tell you what?"

"I've been trying to tell you for years," Nicole continued. "It's okay to date. I'm not going to think that you're cheating on my brother or anything. It's not like that. It's totally—"

"I'm not dating Brody."

Nicole stared at her, a question in her eyes before she tilted her head and grinned. "You can tell me."

"I would. If there was anything to tell." Sarah crossed her arms over her chest. At least, she thought she would. Nicole had become one of her best friends in the last few years, and she told her everything. Well, almost everything. She hadn't told her about the feelings she'd started to have for Brody, the attraction that seemed to be growing more and more every day. Although, clearly, Nicole already thought something was going on. Too bad she was wrong, considering Brody obviously didn't feel the same way about her. She'd also never mentioned to Nicole she was envious of the new relationship butterflies and that she missed the excitement and passion in her life. And she'd definitely never told Nicole that she'd never actually had that with her brother before he'd died.

Sarah sighed. There was a lot she hadn't told Nicole.

"Okay." Nicole smiled. "But I need you to know that it's okay if you were. I'd be happy for you. *Really* happy for you."

"Well, I have a date with Byron Smith."

At least that wasn't a lie. The day after blurting it out to Brody, she'd run into Byron in the grocery store, and he'd once again asked her for a coffee. Sarah had suggested dinner instead. After all, if she was going to try the whole dating thing, she might as well go all in. Maybe an actual date was what she needed to feel like moving on was the right thing after all. There was only one way to find out.

"You have a date?" Nicole's eyes widened in surprise.

Sarah nodded.

"With Byron Smith?"

"He's the dad of one of Rory's soccer friends," Sarah said as way of explanation. "He's asked me a few times and so I finally said yes." Nicole was still looking at her strangely. "You think it's too soon, don't you?"

Her friend shook her head. "Too soon? For what? To date?"

"Yeah."

A moment later, Nicole burst out laughing and for the life of her, Sarah could not see what was so funny. She waited her sister-in-law out until, finally, Nicole's laughter died down.

"Oh," she said. "You were serious."

Sarah tipped her head and groaned. "Yes. I was serious. I've never dated anyone besides Josh and...well..."

"It is *not* too soon, Sarah. It's been almost six years. And I literally just told you that you should start dating. Did you miss all that?" Nicole tucked her hands into her back pockets. "Josh wouldn't have wanted you to be alone. As Josh's older sister, I think I'm in a unique position to tell you exactly what he would or wouldn't want. And he would definitely want you to be happy."

She nodded as she let Nicole pull her into a quick hug.

Despite how sure Nicole was, Sarah couldn't be sure her moving on was what Josh would have wanted. If the last conversation they'd had was any indication...well...it didn't matter anymore. At least that's what she was desperately trying to convince herself of.

"But you looked kind of surprised," Sarah finally said. "It's okay to tell me the truth, Nic. If you have an issue with me going on a date with Byron, tell me."

"Okay," Nicole said without hesitation. "I have a problem with you going on a date with Byron."

She was not expecting Nicole to be so blunt, and her friend's candor took her off guard. Sarah walked to the edge of the porch before turning back.

But before she could speak, Nicole beat her to it. "My problem is you going out with this Byron guy," Nicole said. "Who—don't get me wrong—is probably a perfectly nice guy," she added quickly. "And if you want to go out with him, I'll happily support you. But please, answer me one question."

Sarah stared at her friend.

"Why on earth are you not going out with Brody?"

"Should be all set now."

Brody looked up from the counter, where he was chopping a bundle of fresh parsley from the herb garden he kept in the small garden behind the restaurant to see Al from Al's Appliance Repairs, the man who'd finally arrived from the city a few hours earlier. Or—as he was starting to think of him—his hero. But that term would only apply if cold air started flowing through the vents once more.

"It's fixed?" He was hopeful when he asked, despite the man's earlier assurance. Before the repair man could answer, Brody heard the familiar whir, followed by a rush of cold air from the ceiling as the air conditioner finally started up again. "Oh, thank God. I was starting to think that we might need to come up with a permanent sauna-themed menu."

"It is pretty warm in here," Al agreed as he dragged a cloth over his red face. The cloth looked unsettlingly like one of his napkins, but with the cold air rushing at him, Brody didn't care. It was a small price to pay. "Sorry it took so long to get out here," Al continued. "With a heat wave like this, we've been pretty busy. These old units just can't keep up. And out-of-town calls just aren't the priority."

"I get that." Brody shrugged. Being in a mountain town three hours out of the big city had a lot of advantages, but it also had a few drawbacks, too. "What do you mean, these old units can't keep up?" The second he asked, Brody wished he hadn't. He wasn't sure how much more bad news he could handle. The expenses of running a restaurant, especially one that needed work, were definitely starting to add up. He wasn't sure how much more his savings account could take.

Al shrugged and pulled out a clipboard. "It's pretty old. At least twenty years, and while it was a good unit—once—if you want to avoid any more potential desert-themed menus, I would strongly suggest upgrading. I can get you into a new one for only five grand."

Five grand? Only!

Brody tried not to react, but no doubt the shock showed on his face. He didn't have five grand. The old unit would have to do. "I think I'll stick with what I've got for now. After all, the summer season in the mountains isn't usually very long."

"True," Al said. "But it's a damn important season, am I right?"

"You're not wrong, Al. But one thing at a time. What's the damage today?"

While he waited, Al finished scribbling on his clipboard, adding up numbers and no doubt adding in a travel fee, and finally handed Brody an invoice in an amount that would have been a nice down payment on a brand-new air conditioner. Reluctantly, Brody wrote a check while he mentally calculated what was left in his dwindling savings account and saw the man out.

He was going to have to figure something out to pad his savings account again. The restaurant was doing well. Locals and tourists alike had embraced Birchwood and of course the extra business catering weddings for Hope and Faith at Ever After was a nice bump to his income. But still, the business had expenses. Many of which he hadn't anticipated when he'd bought it. And a new air conditioner was just another thing on an already long list. He wasn't in trouble. Yet. But if anything else broke, it might be a very different situation.

Brody worked through the lunch rush, and finally when things slowed down, he left Amy in charge of the small kitchen staff and with his front of the house handled more than competently by his manager, he slipped out onto Main Street and into the heat of the July afternoon.

Main Street of Glacier Falls was one of Brody's favorite parts of the town and one of the things that had initially drawn him to moving there. The boulevard was lined with trees and a variety of small shops, all with baskets and planters of flowers decorating their storefronts. It was beautiful, really, and so perfectly small town. There wasn't a big box store to be found anywhere; everywhere you looked, there was character and personality. Many of the businesses had been there for years, but there was one brand-new one, and he was looking forward to checking it out.

The Hub was the vision of Katie Langdon, or maybe it was Katie Banks now. Brody had no idea whether she'd taken her new husband, Damon's, last name. He himself had only just met them earlier that summer, but he'd been honored to cater their wedding celebration a few weeks ago. Lifelong friends who'd grown up in Glacier Falls, the couple had rocked the town with their surprise news that, despite the fact that they'd never dated, they were getting married, within days. Most people were shocked, while others, like Sarah, thought that the couple had always been meant for each other. As it turned out, it had originally been a marriage of convenience, but it hadn't taken either of them long to realize they had feelings for each other, although it had taken a little longer for them to figure it out together.

At the end of the day, it had all worked out and they were now happily married. Damon was some sort of crazy billionaire, and after graduating with her degree, Katie had always had a dream of opening an adventure center to rent and sell outdoor equipment for people who wanted to explore the mountains, but didn't have the means, or the know-how.

Brody opened the door to what had been the old hardware store and was immediately impressed. The Hub was packed. Both with equipment and people. He glanced around and saw Katie with a small group of people, outfitted in backpacks and hiking poles. She pointed at a map and gave instructions as she handed out bear spray. On the other end of the space, Damon pulled mountain bikes off a rack on the wall and handed them down to Logan, Katie's big brother, and just the man he was looking for.

Brody made his way across the room. "Looking good in here," he said to Damon, who greeted him with a wave. "You guys are busy."

"Hey, Brody. Good to see you." Damon handed him a bike. "We are busy. It's been crazy."

"Crazy good though?" Logan asked, jumping into the conversation.

Damon nodded and laughed. "I'm not complaining, that's for sure. And Katie is in her element. Turns out that my wife is not only incredibly beautiful," he grinned, "but very smart, because there was clearly a need for this in Glacier Falls."

"Are you talking about how amazing I am?" Katie joined them, and Damon instantly wrapped his arm around her and pulled her close.

"You know it." He kissed her on the top of her head.

Brody couldn't help but feel a flicker of jealousy for the ease between them. He'd gone his entire adult life without a relationship, by choice mostly, choosing instead to focus on culinary school, working long hours and saving all his cash to finally buy the restaurant he'd dreamed of for so long. Restaurant life wasn't usually conducive to a relationship. But things had changed. *He'd* changed. And then, of course, there was Sarah. She had definitely changed things for him. And now, more than ever, Brody was looking forward to that kind of easy love that Damon and Katie shared.

"I was just telling the guys how busy we've been and how smart my gorgeous wife is for having such a great business idea." Damon's words made Katie blush, but only for a moment before she started telling them exactly how busy they'd been and how much fun she'd had starting the store.

"And I hear you guys want to rent some bikes today?" she finished, looking at Logan.

"I have one," Logan said to his little sister. "But Brody here didn't love the old beat-up one from our shed last time. Do you have a newer one he can try out?"

"Of course. Give me a minute."

While Katie was searching for equipment, the men chatted. It was good to see that Logan had made peace with his new brother-in-law, and they'd become friends now that it was clear that Damon loved Katie and would do anything for her.

Brody's phone buzzed with an incoming text message, and the moment he saw the name on the display, he smiled.

I was thinking of going to the lake on Sunday. Maybe a group? Will you come?

"How do you guys feel about the lake?" Brody asked the men, interrupting their conversation.

"Love the lake."

"The lake is awesome."

"Would feel pretty good in this heat."

"Yes!"

Brody listened to the back-and-forth for a minute before Logan finally looked at him. "Have you been?"

Brody shook his head. He'd heard a lot about Cedar Springs and the lake in the neighboring town, but he'd been too busy to ever get there.

"We should go," Damon chimed in. "Get a group together."

"Yes." Brody raised his phone in way of explanation. "That's exactly what Sarah just said."

The men froze and looked at each other. "Sarah?"

"She suggested the lake?" Logan asked. "Sarah did?"

"She did. Just now. She sent me a text."

The men exchanged glances as Katie returned with a mountain bike for Brody. "What's going on?"

Damon offered the information. "Sarah just texted Brody and—"

"Ohh…" Katie wiggled her eyebrows. "Sarah. So things between the two of you are—"

"The same." Brody cut her off. More and more, it seemed as if their friends thought there was something more going on between the two of them. And it didn't matter how his feelings were changing; if Sarah didn't feel the same way, nothing was ever going to happen anyway. "We're friends," he added to make his point. "Good friends."

Damon and Logan exchanged looks that made it very clear they disagreed, but Katie at least seemed to accept his explanation.

"Whatever you say." She winked. "Anyway, what's up with Sarah?"

Logan answered his sister. "She just texted Brody and suggested getting a group together to go to the lake."

Katie's mouth fell open, but she caught herself quickly. "Sarah suggested that?"

Brody nodded his confirmation, although he had no idea why they were being so strange.

"Okay," Katie said slowly. "Then we should go. All of us."

Brody had finally had enough. "What's going on? Why are you all being weird?"

Katie smiled softly. "You know that Sarah's husband Josh drowned, right?"

Brody nodded but before he could say anything, it hit him in a flash. "Shit." He dropped his head and rubbed at the back of his neck before looking up. "At the lake? *The* lake?" He didn't know why, but he'd always assumed he'd drowned in the ocean, or…well, he didn't know what he actually thought. Except that he probably should have asked. "Shit."

"Shit indeed," Logan said. "And Sarah's never been back to the lake. Ever."

"But it seems like she's ready now," Katie added.

She did seem to be ready. *Maybe she was ready for a lot of changes.* First dating, and now this… Brody lifted his phone and reread the text before quickly typing in his reply.

Of course I'll be there for you.

When he hit Send, he looked up and smiled at his new friends. "Well, I guess it's finally time."

Chapter Five

SARAH PICKED at the wilted lettuce in her salad. There was too much dressing on it. There was always too much dressing on the salads at the Knot. Which was why she always ordered dressing on the side. But she'd been distracted when the waitress came and she'd finally ordered her chicken Caesar salad. And it wasn't Byron, her date, who was distracting her. No, it was the man she'd left standing in her living room with her daughter who occupied her thoughts.

She took another sip of her wine but it tasted bitter on her tongue. As she swallowed it down, she forced herself to focus on the man sitting across from her. It wasn't Byron's fault that when Brody had showed up to her house, freshly showered, he'd smelled of citrus and cedar, a combination that had made something low in her belly tighten. Or that he'd complimented her on her dress and the careful way she'd curled her hair into soft waves. His eyes had lingered a little too long on her as he'd paid her the compliment and Sarah had felt her face flush before she'd turned away. She never should have let him babysit. It wasn't fair. For so many reasons.

She'd tried, but she couldn't stop thinking about what

Nicole had said to her. That it was Brody she should be going on a date with. Her sister-in-law had been genuinely confused that she was going out with Byron when she'd spent the last few months hanging out with Brody.

"But we're just friends," she'd tried to explain to Nicole. "He doesn't think of me like that." She'd carefully left out how she might think of him and the way her stomach flipped and her heart raced when she saw him. Not that it mattered. Brody didn't feel the same way. And even if he did…she wouldn't risk it. She couldn't risk losing him the way she'd lost Josh. Josh had been so much more than her husband. He'd been her best friend. There'd been a lot missing from their relationship on the romantic side, but the one thing they'd shared for sure was their deep friendship. She couldn't lose that again. Which was why she was out with Byron. He was safe in so many ways.

"Sarah?"

She shook her head to clear it as she realized her date had asked her a question.

"Are you okay?"

She nodded and tried to smile. "Sorry, my mind just drifted. I wasn't thinking of…"

"I know how it is." He nodded and smiled kindly.

"You do?"

"I do." Byron reached across the table for her hand and Sarah watched, detached from herself, as she let him cradle it in his. "Dating again after so long can be hard," he said confidently. "And as a single parent, we have so many demands on us, it can be hard to stay focused on the moment, even when it's such a perfect one." He squeezed her hand gently and it was that simple action that snapped her back into the moment.

She pulled her hand away and hoped it didn't look too rude as she tucked it into her lap. "Yes," she lied. "It's all a little crazy." She dropped her gaze to her half-eaten salad and sighed. She closed her eyes for a minute and made a decision.

When she looked up, Sarah could see by the look in Byron's eyes that he knew what she was going to say before she even said it. "Byron, I'm sorry. I shouldn't have agreed to come on a date with you tonight." She tried to smile. He really was a nice guy. He just wasn't the guy for her.

Brody is the guy for you. Her stupid internal voice was yelling at her, but it wasn't the time or place for her to pay it any mind. Especially because it was wrong.

"I'm not going to lie," Byron said. "I was surprised when you said yes." He chuckled a little. "Please—don't get me wrong. But I didn't really think you were interested."

She sighed. "You're a really great guy."

He shook his head and took a sip of his beer. "I sense a but coming."

"I really am sorry." Sarah shrugged. "This is all new to me."

"Honestly, Sarah. Don't be sorry." He offered her a small smile. "Dating after divorce is hard enough. I can't imagine your situation. I get it."

And even though Byron couldn't possibly really *get* it completely, the fact that he might, even just a little bit, made Sarah feel better.

"Besides that," he continued. "I always thought there was something going on with you and Brody."

She almost choked on the sip of wine she'd just taken and it took her a few moments to recover.

Did everyone think there was something between her and Brody?

"Brody and I are good friends." She reached for her wine and tried another sip. This time, the pressure of the evening lifted, the crispness of the sauvignon blanc was cold and fruity on her tongue. "And he's a great coach for our girls, isn't he?" She transitioned into a safer subject. "What do you think of their little soccer season? It's been pretty awesome. And the final game with Cedar Springs will be a good one."

They spent the rest of the evening on safer subjects as they discussed their girls, their jobs, and life in Glacier Falls. By the time their *date* wrapped up, they were both on the same page. They'd discovered a new friend in the other, but that was as far as it would go.

More importantly for Sarah was the spark of a different realization that had only become clearer as the night went on. Her feelings for Brody were more than just friendly, no matter how much she tried to tell herself otherwise. And it scared the hell out of her.

Brody wiped the kitchen counters for the fourth time. All traces of the bedtime snack he'd prepared for Rory were long gone. Still, he wiped. Maybe it was his time in culinary school, or years working in restaurants, but Brody cleaned when he was restless. It was usually a surefire way for him to calm his nerves and still his thoughts.

Except tonight.

He glanced at the clock over Sarah's pantry again. It was almost nine. She should be home soon.

Unless the date went well.

Maybe they'd stay all night. Talking and—

No.

He wouldn't let his mind go there. *To kissing or—*

No. Definitely he wasn't going to let his mind go *there*.

The idea of Sarah kissing or doing anything at all with any man would make him crazy. He never should have agreed to babysit. Hell, he never should have offered. But he couldn't stop himself. All week, since those words slipped out of his mouth, he'd wanted to take them back. It was bad enough that Sarah was going on a date with another man, but to *help* her do it? To sit and wait in her house for her to come home and tell him all about what it was like to date another man?

He should have his head examined.

Brody grabbed the bottle of cleaner and left another layer of mist on the counter. He attacked it with ferocity.

It had been easier not to think of why he was babysitting when Rory was awake. They'd kicked the soccer ball in the backyard before coming inside to a snack of apple slices and cheese before he'd let her show him all of her stuffed animals. He now knew that Lucky the frog was her favorite, followed by Clara, an old teddy bear. Of course, there was also Bramble the bunny that had the place of pride on her bed. It was Bramble that she'd wrapped her little arm around and snuggled close as he'd read her no fewer than four bedtime stories before she'd finally drifted to sleep.

He'd watched for a minute to make sure she was really asleep before slipping out of the room and flicking the light off and leaving the door ajar a little, just the way she'd instructed him.

Brody had never thought about having children of his own. Of course, he'd also never thought that he would end up in a small mountain town, best friends with a single mom of a little girl, and quite possibly falling in love with both of them even though that single mom was out on a date with another man and clearly didn't feel the same way about him that he felt about her. Probably because he'd been too big of a chicken shit to say anything at all.

Dammit.

He scrubbed the counter harder but the sound of a car pulling up distracted him from his job. Brody dropped the sponge in the sink and moved to the side of the window to see Byron's SUV pull up in front of the house. Sarah had driven herself to the pub. *Was Byron coming in for a nightcap?* He wasn't sure he could handle that. It was one thing sitting in her house while she was on a date with the man. It was a totally different thing to watch him waltz in to her living room as if he belonged there. *Hell.* Brody belonged there. A surge of jealousy rose up through his body and he had to force himself to close his eyes and take a deep breath. He had no right to be jealous. None at all.

But that didn't mean he wasn't.

He exhaled slowly and opened his eyes at the sound of voices coming up the walk. As subtly as he could, he drew the lemon-printed kitchen curtain to the side. Not a lot, but just enough that he could see Sarah and Byron.

They stood close together. He said something that made her smile. And then she laughed. And touched his arm. Byron leaned in…and…they hugged.

They hugged.

Brody exhaled a long breath.

What was happening to him? He would have laughed at his behavior if it hadn't taken him so completely off guard. He'd never behaved in such a way.

Because you've never cared.

Not like this.

Brody dropped the curtain and picked up the sponge again. The front door opened and he heard Sarah say good-bye before the door closed again. Brody pretend to scrub the spotless counter as she came into the adjoining kitchen.

"Oh." He feigned surprise. "You're home already."

She tilted her head a little before giving it a little shake. "I am." Sarah moved to the cupboard, retrieved a glass, and got herself a glass of water all while Brody kept scrubbing at the counter.

"Byron drove me home," she added. "I had a little too much wine at dinner. I was afraid it might have gone to my head. I'll grab my car in the morning."

"He didn't come in?"

"No."

"It didn't go well?" Brody knew he was playing with fire, but he couldn't seem to stop himself. He stopped scrubbing for a minute and looked up. She stood directly across from him, watching him with a small smile on her face.

"It went fine."

"I thought maybe he'd come in for a nightcap."

"Why would you think that?"

"Isn't that how dates go?"

"Is it?" She put her glass of water down and jumped up to sit on the kitchen island. Her bare legs dangled over the edge. "I guess I wouldn't know," she continued. "That's the first date I've been on since I was seventeen." She tipped her head and winked at him. "Did I do it wrong?"

Was she flirting with him?

Every part of him was on high alert. A low vibration started to thrum through his body. "No," he said slowly. "I think you did it just right."

"By sending him home?" She leaned back on her arms, which had the very desirable effect of pushing her breasts out against the thin material of her sundress. *Damn.* "That was the right dating protocol?"

She was definitely flirting with him.

Brody had to swallow back a low growl that threatened to escape from deep inside him. Before he could answer her, she lifted an eyebrow in the direction of his sponge and the counter he was still scrubbing at. "Did you make a mess of things?"

She had no idea.

"You could say that." His voice was low and rough. Brody tossed the sponge aside and crossed the short distance to stand in front of Sarah. He'd had way too much of the distance between them. And maybe he was reading things wrong. Maybe he'd always been reading things wrong. But he didn't care. If sitting around in her house while she went out on a date had taught him anything, it was that he knew exactly what he wanted. And it was his best friend.

And he hoped like hell she wanted him too.

He reached out to brush her long, dark hair from her bare shoulder. The touch of her skin sent a shock through him, and he didn't miss the way her body shuddered, ever so slightly. "I've made a huge mess of things." He lowered his voice as he let his thumb gently stroke her cheek. Her eyes closed and a small sigh escaped her lips before she once more looked at him. When their eyes locked, he knew he hadn't misread a thing. "But it's nothing I can't fix." He spoke the words as he took his chance and leaned in.

He was going to kiss her.

Brody was going to kiss her.

Sarah's entire body went into full alert.

It also went into full betrayal mode by lighting up like a freakin' Christmas tree at the prospect.

Her body wanted his lips on hers.

Her brain...well...*hell.*

Right before his lips touched hers, she scooted to the side of the counter and hopped down. "I'm hungry." She opened the fridge and stuck her head inside, using the cool air to calm her and give her a minute to think. "The salads at the Knot are never any good."

"Sarah?"

She ignored him and took another breath.

"Sarah, I didn't...well...I'm—"

She grabbed a container of yogurt and spun around in time to stop him from apologizing. "Don't," she said. "Please don't apologize for...well, for whatever it was that was just about to happen."

"A kiss."

He took a step toward her, but thankfully kept his distance. She didn't know whether she was going to be able to stay strong if he came any closer because *damn* did he ever smell good and every single cell in her body was screaming out to reverse time and let his lips press to hers. It had been so long since she'd been kissed. *So long.*

"A kiss was about to happen," he continued. "And I think I really should apologize. I…" He ran a hand through his thick hair and it took up in all different adorable angles. He chuckled a little. "I guess I just read that situation wrong. I thought maybe you—"

"I do. I mean, I did. I mean…I don't know what I mean." She held the yogurt in her hands and stared at it. "I'm so confused," she said honestly.

"About yogurt?" He teased. "It's just a snack. Not a life-or-death decision."

She couldn't help it; Sarah smiled and lifted her gaze. Brody was watching her with a kind smile.

"It's just a snack," he repeated.

She laughed. A second later, the tears came, confusing her even more.

She felt Brody move closer, and then his arms were around her, holding her close. He took the yogurt cup from her hand and hugged her tight.

"It's just yogurt," he said. "There are enough things in life to cry over. Yogurt just isn't worth it."

His words were meant to make her laugh, and they did. But they almost made her cry harder. Sarah wasn't a crier— she rarely let her emotions loose so recklessly—but for the life of her, she couldn't seem to stop crying. And even crazier, she couldn't decide whether she was crying over yogurt or Brody or something else entirely.

"Sarah?" Brody's voice was laced with concern. "Look at me," he demanded. "Please."

She left the comfortable security of his chest and lifted her head so she looked in his eyes. Through the blur of her tears, she saw the worry on his face. The care and concern. And *love*.

Before she could convince herself otherwise, she lifted herself up on her tiptoes and pressed her lips to his.

It was sweet and soft and also…everything but.

Sarah let herself melt into the kiss. He pulled her closer and cupped her cheek, and it all felt so completely perfect. And for a moment, she let herself believe that it really could be. But then, reality crashed through all the *maybes* and she pulled away.

She felt the absence of him acutely and instantly. But still, she turned away. "I shouldn't have done that," she mumbled. "I'm sorry. That wasn't fair." She moved to walk away but he grabbed her hand and held her fast.

"That was perfectly fair." Brody's voice was low and gravelly in a way she'd never heard before. "I'm not complaining, Sarah," he added. "But if you walk away, I don't—"

"I have to walk away." Sarah turned and looked directly at him. Her tears had dried now, but the wild ride of emotions was still slamming through her. "Brody, we can't do this."

"We can."

"No." She shook her head, resolute. "You're my best friend and up until a few minutes ago, I didn't even think you felt that way about me and now…well, I can't lose you, too." She exhaled slowly. "I just can't."

He was silent for a moment but then he nodded without releasing his hold on her hand. "Okay," he said. "If you say we can't do this, then we can't. I'm not going to pressure you. But without knowing what the hell you're talking about, I'm going to say this."

She waited a breath before he continued.

"We absolutely *can* do this. And you are *not* going to lose me."

The weight of her secret was heavy on her heart. It had been over five years, and she'd never told anyone about what had happened at the lake that day. She'd never told another living soul why Josh had gone for a swim that day. And why she'd lost him. Sarah exhaled slowly and looked directly into Brody's eyes.

"I lost my best friend once before, Brody, and it almost killed me, too."

"Sarah, nothing is going to happen to me."

She smiled sadly. "You don't know that."

"No," he said. "I guess I don't. Not with absolute certainty." He took a step closer. "But, Sarah, you can't live your life scared that an accident will—"

"It wasn't an accident." She blurted out the words, but the moment they were out, it was as if a weight had lifted.

"You already told me there was no child he was trying to save. But still, it was an accident, Sarah."

"No," she said again. "I let everyone believe what they wanted about the child. That's true," she continued. "But that's not everything."

He watched her with question in his eyes, but to his credit, didn't rush her. Sarah looked down for a moment. It would be so easy not to say anything more. It would be so easy to continue to keep her secret.

But it would be so much easier just to tell the truth. She swallowed hard and looked up. "It was my fault," she said softly. "Josh's death was my fault."

Had he just heard her right?

Brody was sure he'd misunderstood what Sarah had just

said. He had to have misheard. He chuckled a little, but she didn't smile. "What do you mean?" he asked more seriously. "How was it your fault? I thought it was a drowning."

She looked so sad and broken in that moment, but Brody had the instinct not to touch her. Whatever it was that she was saying to him was taking her a lot of courage. She needed to stand on her own. It took her a moment, but Sarah finally spoke.

"He had no intention to go swimming that day. It was too cold." She shook her head. "It was only June. The ice was barely even off the water. In fact, we were only at the lake because I'd suggested going for a picnic. I needed to get out of town and have a change of scenery. I was hoping that it would…" Her fingers floated to her lips and she squeezed her eyes shut for a second before opening them again. "I was hoping that what I had to tell him would be easier if we weren't at home." She shook her head. "I was wrong. Maybe it was even harder. And then…"

"Hey." He reached out then and took her hand. "Whatever it was you had to say to him, it wasn't your fault. What happened to Josh, it was an accident, Sarah. You know that."

"No." She took a breath. "He was upset. He ran off before I could stop him and then…the next thing I knew, he was in the lake. He was swimming and swimming. And it wasn't that he wasn't a strong swimmer," she continued. "Because he was. He was a great swimmer. But the water was cold and he just kept going. The investigators think that maybe he went out too far and couldn't get back, or maybe it was a cramp because of the water temperature." She took a deep breath. "But I'm not sure they're right."

"What are you saying?"

She looked him straight in the eyes, and he could see how much it was costing her to tell him what had obviously been weighing on her for so long. "I can't be sure if he meant to come back or not."

He absorbed what she'd just said. "Do you think maybe he…"

"Kept swimming on purpose." She answered his unfinished question and nodded slightly. "I've always wondered. And I just can't be sure."

Brody looked at her and for the first time saw the toll that her past had taken on her. She looked exhausted, as if she were only being held up by sheer will. She was too special, too kind and loving and giving to have to concern herself with such thoughts. He couldn't even imagine her back then. A young woman, only barely married and with a new baby in her arms, she had her whole life ahead of her. She should never have had to think for one second that her husband might have killed himself. Because of something she had said.

"Sarah," his voice was soft and he squeezed her hand to give her strength, "I can't imagine anything you could have said would have driven him to hurt himself or to intentionally put himself in danger. It just doesn't—"

"I told him I wanted a divorce."

Silence filled the space around them, making the air in the kitchen feel thick and heavy. A tear slipped down her cheek, and Brody longed to reach forward and wipe it away. Instead, he took her other hand in his. Gently, and wordlessly, he led her out of the kitchen and onto the living room couch.

"I've never told anyone that before," she said once they were settled. "No one knew I was unhappy. No one knew that our marriage was loveless." She chuckled a little, but there was no humor in it. "And really, that's not totally fair." She shook her head. "It wasn't loveless."

Sarah blinked hard and Brody could see the struggle on her face as she tried to make sense of what she was saying. He waited patiently for her to continue.

"I loved Josh very much," she said after a few moments. "And I miss him every day." She blew out a deep breath. "But there was something missing from our relationship. There always had been. It wasn't..." She stopped herself and shook her head again before looking at him. "Do you ever find that sometimes you can look at a couple and you can just see, by the way they look at each other and the way they touch each other, how in love they are?"

"Absolutely." He knew exactly what she was talking about because it described almost every single couple he knew in Glacier Falls.

She pressed her lips together and nodded once.

"Ah, I see. And you didn't have that."

It wasn't a question, but she nodded anyway. "I think we were just together so long that a love grew between us, but it wasn't the same kind of *can't keep your hands off each other, desperately passionate* love that I saw around me. It was the easy companionship type of love. A deep friendship with absolutely none of the other stuff. In fact, we'd barely even kissed since Rory was born. Let alone had sex." She shrugged. "And maybe I was being selfish and terrible and all the things, but I wanted more." She closed her eyes and tipped her head back.

In that moment, Brody could see how much the truth had weighed on her. Sarah had been a young woman, her whole life ahead of her, and all she'd wanted was a little passion. She wasn't terrible or horrible but completely normal. But she couldn't seem to see that.

Brody reached out and put his hand on her thigh. He squeezed gently, a move that was meant to be supportive, but she scooted away just slightly and kept talking.

"When I told him that we were best friends and I valued that more than anything, but that we both deserved to be with someone who made us feel all the things, he wouldn't hear it. He got so upset and said that it was a mistake and we couldn't break up our family and that he loved me." A tear slipped down her cheek. "He yelled and told me I was making a huge, irreparable mistake and if I insisted on leaving him, I'd lose him completely. That I couldn't have it both ways."

Brody swallowed hard, knowing what was coming next.

"I insisted it was the right thing," Sarah said. "I'd thought about it for years. Before Rory was even born. And I wasn't going to change my mind." She lifted her head and looked at him. "I'll never forget the look on his face when he realized my mind was made up. But I couldn't take it back, Brody. I *knew* it was the right thing for both of us, and the crazy thing is, I'm absolutely sure he knew it too. He just needed time. He would have come to agree with me, I *know* it. And we would have been the best co-parents around. Best friends, doing the best thing for Rory, and each other." She smiled a little at the idea, but it was short-lived. "But I didn't get that chance, because he took off, and before I could even get Rory into the stroller and follow him, he was already in the lake. I yelled at him. But he either didn't hear me or ignored me. I thought he'd come back, Brody." More tears slipped down her face.

He handed her the box of tissues and she blew her nose.

"I never thought he wouldn't come back. I mean, he was such a strong swimmer and...well. It doesn't matter, because he didn't come back." Her shoulders sagged. "And I'll never know what could have been with us. And worse, I'll never know if he meant to or not."

She completely crumpled then and Brody couldn't hold off any longer; he moved so he could pull her into his arms and he held her tight while she cried. In all the time he'd known Sarah, he'd barely seen her shed a tear. She was a strong woman and she held herself together without barely a crack, but even knowing that, it didn't surprise him to watch the outpouring of emotion. There was only so much one woman could take, strong or not, and Sarah had more than her fair share.

He didn't know how long they sat like that, but it didn't matter. Brody would have stayed that way, holding her tight against him, his T-shirt soaked through from her tears, as long as it took if it meant he could take away even a little bit of the pain that she'd been holding for so long.

He rubbed a small circle on her back. "Sarah, it's not your fault. You can't know what happened out there, but I can't imagine he would have...well, I didn't know Josh, but there's no way he would have left you and Rory that way. Not on purpose."

She sniffed hard and pulled back a little. "Don't you get it, Brody?"

He shook his head.

"It's my fault. No matter what happened out there in the lake," she said with so much sadness in her voice it caused Brody physical pain. "He never would have been there if it wasn't for me. He never would have gone for a swim if I hadn't selfishly wanted more. I ruined everything. *Everything.* In such a completely and terribly permanent way. And all because I wanted more."

He knew where she was going with her line of thinking, and it didn't matter if it didn't make sense; it made sense to her. Brody shook his head and opened his mouth to stop her but she beat him to it.

"I won't do it again," she said. "I won't lose what I already have because I think I need more. Not again."

"No."

"Brody, don't. Please, I—"

"Sarah, this is crazy." Brody moved so he faced her and took both her hands in his. He squeezed them and brought them to his lips as he spoke. "You are worthy and deserving of so much more. You should have *everything* you ever wanted. You deserve it all. And I know this terrible, horrible thing happened, Sarah. But it isn't your fault and you need to stop blaming yourself and let yourself live. I care about you, Sarah. You're not going to lose me."

She closed her eyes and, for a moment, Brody thought maybe he'd gotten through to her.

But when she opened them again, she had a small smile on her face. "You're right, I'm not going to lose you, because we can never be anything more than friends. Best friends," she added quickly. "But just friends." She shook her head and got to her feet. "I know this is confusing." She chuckled a little. "Hell, it is for me too. Up until about twenty minutes ago, I didn't even know you thought of me like that, and maybe that was easier because now knowing…well, it all seems a little too real and I just don't think I can handle anything else. Please understand."

He didn't. He didn't even come close to understanding what she was saying, but Brody knew enough to know that if he pushed it, he'd push her away. After a moment, he nodded. "Okay." He swallowed hard. "Friends."

Even as Brody said it, he didn't know how the hell he was going to manage to keep his feelings for Sarah in check. Not after that kiss. Not now that everything he was feeling for her was growing so quickly and gaining strength by the second. But if it was what Sarah needed, then that's what he would do.

Friends.

At least, for the time being.

Chapter Six

BAG OF TOWELS. *Check.*

Sand toys. *Check.*

Umbrella. *Check.*

Tote bag with enough sunscreen for an army. *Check.*

Cooler full of cold drinks. *Check.*

Folding chairs. *Check.*

Sarah stood back and examined the pile of essentials she'd put by the door.

The only thing she didn't have was a cooler full of food, but Brody had insisted he'd take care of lunch and snacks, and considering she was enough of a stress case without having to worry about preparing food that wouldn't go bad in the heat, she'd readily agreed.

Brody.

It had been three days since they'd kissed.

And since she'd pushed him away.

And worse...or maybe better...told him *everything*.

Sarah had never told anyone about that day and what really happened. She'd never told anyone about her feelings for Josh and what she'd longed for. Not one person. How could she? They'd hate her. Nicole would blame her for her brother's death. Her father would never look at her the same way and everyone around town...well...no. It had just been better to let everyone think that they were desperately in love and that he had been the love of her life. A hero who'd had a terrible accident.

She should have felt panicked that her secret was now out there for the whole world to potentially discover. After all, she hadn't specifically told Brody not to tell anyone. It was kind of unspoken, but still...there was nothing stopping him from telling someone. And if he did...

He wouldn't.

She knew it in her heart. That was why she'd been ready to unload it all. And even though she'd meant the truth to act like a wall to keep Brody at arm's length, she'd felt closer to him ever since. Sarah knew he was just being respectful to her by agreeing to be friends. He probably thought she had completely lost it, especially after she'd kissed him. But she'd meant what she'd said. She couldn't lose him too. It had all become perfectly clear with one kiss.

And she'd meant it when she'd said it. But that was only a few days ago and despite how absolutely sure she'd been at the time, her resolve was already weakening. Every time she closed her eyes, she could remember the feel of his lips on hers. The scent of him filling her senses, the taste of him and how such a small, simple kiss had awakened something in her that she had never felt before. *Never.*

Sarah released a long breath. No matter what it was she thought she was feeling, now wasn't the time to let herself go down that rabbit hole. After all, she had stuff to do, because Brody would be arriving soon and there were only minutes left before she got ready to face the scene of Josh's death for the first time.

Mentally, Sarah chastised herself. *What was wrong with her?*

The last thing she should be thinking of was how her deceased husband never made her feel the way Brody did and how badly she wanted him to kiss her again.

She shook her head and tried to focus on what was about to happen.

Sarah once more looked over the pile of things by the door. She had everything they could possibly need for a trip to the beach.

It will be fine.

She took another breath and told herself again.

It will be fine.

It was like a mantra she seemed to have on constant repeat.

What if it wasn't fine?

Before she could stop it, the panic crept in.

What if she got there and it was all too much? What if Rory remembered? That was dumb. She'd only been a baby; she'd never remember that day. *But what if she felt it? What if Rory could feel her dad's spirit there? What if she could? What if they went in the water and—*

Sarah shook her head and forced herself to stay calm. She could not let herself get worked up with the *what-ifs*.

It will be fine.

She slowed her breathing and repeated the words until finally she believed them.

Standing on Nicole's porch earlier in the week, she'd been emboldened and it had all seemed like a good idea. A day at the beach. Fun. No problem. After all, her sister-in-law was right—she couldn't avoid the lake forever. Especially on a hot summer day.

Still.

Maybe it hadn't been a good idea.

Sarah leaned against the wall and covered her face with her hands.

"Knock, knock."

She pushed up with a jump and fiddled with her T-shirt as Brody walked through the screen door.

"You okay?" He raised an eyebrow and watched her carefully for a moment. "What's going on?"

She nodded and shook her head all at once, the action making her laugh. "Yes, I'm okay and no, nothing's going on." She was lying and they both knew it.

He leaned in and moved to give her a kiss on the cheek, but before he could, she quickly stepped back and put distance between them.

Brody raised an eyebrow, but didn't say anything as he glanced down the hall.

"She's getting ready," Sarah said.

Brody nodded, his eyebrows raised as he took in the pile of things she'd gathered. "Do you think you have enough stuff?" He chuckled and shook his head so he missed the way she rolled her eyes.

"To be fair," Sarah said in defense of herself, "it's been awhile. I don't really know what I'll…" Her thought drifted away as tears suddenly pricked at her eyes. "I'm okay." She nodded, willing herself to believe it. The truth was, she'd barely slept the night before. Sarah had never considered herself an anxious person. Even after Josh died, she'd never suffered from any kind of anxiety. Which was why it was so ridiculous that she was worked up about a day at the beach with her friends. It would be fine. Everything would be fine.

Brody pulled her in for a quick hug.

She melted into the feel of him and at once felt stronger just for his presence.

"It's okay to be stressed about this, you know? It's a big deal. It might not be an easy day." He kissed her on the top of her head and smiled. "But I'm here for it. I'm here for you, Sarah. It'll be okay and I'm willing to bet that we're actually going to have a good time."

Something about the way he said it actually made her believe it. She nodded a little but before she could respond, Rory ran into the room and Sarah took an instinctive step away from Brody.

"We're going to the beach!" She screeched in that high-pitched way that little girls had and spun in a dramatic circle, showing off her outfit.

"Wow." Sarah pulled out of Brody's arms and held her hand to her mouth to keep from laughing. "You sure look ready."

"Right?" Rory spun again. "Do you like it?"

She wore a sunshine-yellow one-piece swimsuit with large purple polka dots adorning it. It was perfectly bright and ridiculous. On her head was a floppy straw hat and oversized white sunglasses.

"Where did you get all that?" Sarah shook her head as she asked the question she already knew the answer to.

"Auntie Nicole! Do you like it?" She spun yet again, her little arms out at her side as she did so.

"I love it." Sarah pulled her into a quick hug before handing her the bag of sand toys. "Let's get going before I change my mind."

She realized her mistake as soon as the words came out of her mouth.

"Why would you change your mind, Mommy?" Rory looked at her with such innocence it threatened to break her heart. "I've always wanted to go to the beach."

Sarah stared at her daughter and smiled. It *was* going to be a hard day. But it was also going to be a good one.

"You're going to have a great time," she said and looked to Brody. "It's going to be a good day."

Brody winked in support. "Damn right it will."

As Rory bent down to gather up the towels in her arms, Brody caught Sarah's gaze again, and mouthed the words, "I got you."

Her stomach flipped a little, and Sarah couldn't help but hope like hell that he was right.

It had taken most of the day, but Brody was happy to see that Sarah had finally started to relax at the lake. It helped that so many of her friends had come out to share the day with her. They occupied a decent chunk of the beach and the grassy area that sat under the giant leafy trees. Brody recognized most of the faces, but there were a few new ones, too.

All around him, people were swimming, building sandcastles, reading, sleeping, and even playing a particularly cutthroat game of beach volleyball.

From his spot on their blanket, Brody glanced across the crowd to see Sarah and Rory building a sandcastle with Katie. He couldn't help but notice that they'd set up farther away from the water's edge than he would have thought practical. Katie was making all the trips with the bucket to collect water, but it looked as if both Sarah and Rory were having a good time. And that was really all that mattered.

Now, knowing what he knew about what had happened the last time Sarah and Rory had been to the beach, he was a little more sensitive with her. Okay, a lot more. She had some hard memories to deal with, that much was for sure, but he was determined to change that for her. At least in a small way.

Brody looked past them to where his chef Amy was lying on a blanket, quite closely, to Sarah's sister-in-law. He couldn't help but smile. Amy hadn't been very forthright about their relationship, but there was no denying that something was going on between them. The way they each leaned up on an elbow, looking at the other, it was pretty clear that whatever was going on between them was stronger than a simple friendship.

Maybe love was really in the air.

He thought again to his kiss the other night with Sarah. Nothing about that night had been planned. Hell, nothing with Sarah had been planned.

Sarah herself hadn't been planned.

And it definitely hadn't been part of the plan for Sarah to confess the secret that had been weighing on her for five years, let alone the admission that she was fully prepared to deny herself the happiness that she deserved as some sort of misguided punishment for it.

He'd be patient with her. He had no other choice. Especially now that he knew that she had feelings for him too. As screwed up as it all was, there would be time to figure it all out. Besides, he'd waited this long to have a relationship; he could wait a little longer. Brody had never considered having an actual relationship before, not in any serious way. It's not that he was a player who didn't want to settle down, not at all. It was more that he'd had other priorities. And those priorities hadn't changed when he moved to Glacier Falls and bought Birchwood. If anything, they'd only grown more important. He'd invested every single cent he'd saved into that restaurant. He had to make it work. There was no back-up plan. A relationship was even less on the radar than before.

Then he'd met Sarah and Rory.

He wasn't sure who'd stolen his heart first, but when he'd seen them in the park next to the waterfall in town, kicking a soccer ball back and forth in the newly fallen snow, something had shifted. He'd gone over to join them; after all, he was new to town, and he didn't know, maybe playing soccer in the snow was a thing in Glacier Falls. Rory had agreed right away to let him play with them, but Sarah had been a little more hesitant, as a good mom should be. After all, he was a complete stranger. Somehow he'd convinced her that he was harmless, and when Rory, who'd readily confessed that she'd only recently decided to be a professional soccer player, heard that he used to play with his high school team, Sarah didn't have much choice than to let him play with them.

Over the next few weeks of seeing them around town, and discovering that they had some mutual friends, things between them started to develop too. Into a friendship, obviously. But a strong one. And somewhere along the line, his feelings started to change. It had happened slowly, probably because it was the last thing he'd been looking for. He never had a great role model for relationships growing up, and it was just never a priority. After all, why would you want to get involved with someone who you fought with all the time, like his parents? But with Sarah, it was different. They had fun together and laughed and played. They complemented each other. And even before the other night, Brody honestly couldn't imagine his life without her daily text messages, quick chats on the phone, and shared dinners.

He couldn't imagine his life without her.

Was that how Sarah felt? Was that why she wasn't willing to ruin what they had by wanting more?

Damn.

The thought hit him hard, because no matter what she'd said about not wanting more than a friendship with him, he knew she was lying. She *did* want more. She just wouldn't let herself have it. And he wanted more. *They* should be having more.

And they would.

Brody had to force himself to take a deep breath and slow down. He'd promised her he wouldn't push it. He'd promised her nothing but friendship. And he wouldn't break that promise.

Not until she was ready.

It was definitely not going to be easy. Not after that kiss, as innocent as it had been.

No. As innocent as it *should* have been. He chuckled at himself and the circumstance he'd found himself in.

"What's so funny?"

Brody looked over his shoulder, pulled from his thoughts by the arrival of Logan Langdon, who dropped down on the beach blanket next to him. He handed him a beer, which Brody accepted with a smile.

"I was just thinking about a few things," he replied, trying and failing to keep his gaze from Sarah, who'd retreated to the shade to sit with Faith.

"Interesting," Logan said, after taking a swallow of beer. "Your thoughts must be a whole lot funnier than mine." He nudged Brody with his elbow and they both laughed. "Or maybe it's a certain lady friend putting you in such a good mood."

Brody turned to the other man. "Lady friend?" He shook his head. "I didn't realize you'd turned eighty overnight."

"Touché." Logan lifted his beer can in salute. "So what is going on between the two of you anyway? I've heard rumors."

It didn't surprise Brody. There'd been rumors about the two of them for months. The fact that maybe some of those rumors might actually have some truth to them now made him happier—and more frustrated—than he cared to admit. "Can I tell you something, Logan?" He turned to his friend, suddenly serious. Logan nodded and Brody continued. "I really like her."

"You don't say?" Logan rolled his eyes.

"No." Brody shook his head. "I *really* like her."

"Yeah, I get that." Logan laughed. "It's not news. But the real question is, what's actually going on between the two of you? Are things…"

Brody nodded and then shook his head. He couldn't tell

Logan the truth. Sarah had confided in him, and he wasn't going to betray that. Ultimately, he just shrugged. "It's complicated with Sarah."

Logan nodded knowingly. "Like the fact that we're sitting at the very spot where her—"

"Brody?"

Both men turned their heads to see Rory, an inflatable duck life ring around her waist. With her bright-yellow and purple polka dot swimsuit, she was very bright. And very cute.

"What's up, kiddo?"

Rory looked as if she might burst into tears at any moment, but she straightened her spine and crossed her little arms over the yellow duck head. "Mom won't let me go swimming and it's so hot."

Oh. Brody looked to Logan, who shook his head and gave him a look that made it clear he wasn't going to be any help.

"I'm sure your mom has a good reason, kiddo."

Yeah, a very good reason.

Rory shook her head. "She doesn't. She just said no." Her lower lip started to tremble. "It's not fair. Those kids are swimming." She pointed to the swim area that was in fact full of kids splashing on inflatable rafts, throwing beach balls, or jumping from the wooden raft that was anchored farther out. "It's not fair."

Brody had to admit it wasn't fair. But he knew what Sarah's reasons were. He also knew that maybe he could help.

"I'll tell you what," Brody said to Rory. "Why don't I go talk to your mom? I'm not making any promises," he added. "But maybe I can figure out what she's thinking."

Rory nodded in agreement when Logan chimed in. "Can you show me the sandcastle you've been building with my little sister? Did you know that Katie and I used to make sandcastles together when we were your age? She got all her best building techniques from me."

Rory looked amazed to think that Logan or Katie could have ever been as young as she was. And she happily led Logan away to show him her handiwork.

Brody watched them for a minute before picking himself up off the blanket, dusting off the sand and going in search of Sarah.

"I know what you're going to say," Sarah said the moment Brody got close enough. She was sitting with Faith in the shade of an umbrella, and up until a few minutes ago, when Rory came to beg her to go swimming, she would have said that their beach day had been a success. But a pouting child was never a success. Especially when she couldn't explain to her *why* she didn't want her to go swimming. "And I don't want to hear it."

"And what do you think I'm going to say?" Brody stood in front of them.

Despite herself, Sarah couldn't help but trail her eyes up the length of him. He looked damn good in his swim shorts. His too pale chest glistened in the sun from the layer of sunscreen she'd helped him apply earlier. No way did she want him to put a T-shirt on to cover those muscles. She had no idea he was in such good shape. He looked as though he spent his days in the gym. But she'd never once heard of him actually working out or could imagine when he'd ever have time to do it.

She swallowed hard and focused on what he was asking. "You're going to tell me that I should let Rory go swimming."

Next to her, Faith cleared her throat loudly and stood. "I don't think this is any of my business." She smiled. "Besides that, it really is hot and I'm going to cool off." She shot Sarah an apologetic glance as she took off in her tiny bikini down the beach.

Reflexively, Sarah sucked in her stomach and adjusted her position on the blanket. She hadn't been comfortable in her body in a long time, and sitting in front of the man she was ridiculously attracted to, wearing a bathing suit while surrounded by the perfect bodies of all her friends, wasn't doing much for her self-esteem.

But she had bigger problems than her body image for the moment.

"I am going to tell you that." Brody knelt on the sand in front of her. "It's a beautiful day and we are at the beach, after all."

She shook her head. "I can't." Since arriving at the lake, Sarah had done her best to avoid the spot just to the left of where the rope was tied off to mark the swim area. The place where they'd pulled out Josh's body and performed CPR. The spot she'd last seen him. But now, with Brody there, her eyes naturally moved along the shoreline to the very place it had all happened.

Brody turned and followed her gaze.

Of course, there was nothing to see, but Sarah could see it as if it were happening all over again right in front of her. The useless efforts of the first responders when they all knew he was already gone.

Brody moved until he sat next to her. He wrapped an arm around her and pulled her tight to him.

The warmth of his skin on hers felt good and it warmed her through, despite the fact that she hadn't been cold; his embrace filled a spot deep inside her.

"It was there," he said quietly. It wasn't a question, but she nodded. "Do you want to talk about it?"

She did. But at the same time, she really didn't.

Sarah swallowed hard. "I know I should let her go swimming," she said after a moment. "She doesn't understand and she never should have to. She's a kid." She took a deep breath and sat a little straighter. Brody still didn't move his arm, a gesture she was grateful for. "But I don't know if I can do it, Brody. I don't know if I'm…" Her words trailed away.

Brody turned so he faced her and brushed a loose strand of hair from her face. He smelled of a mixture of coconut sun lotion and the salty sun-drenched scent that came from spending the day outside. It was sexy and refreshing and comforting all at the same time. "You're very strong," he said softly, finishing her thought. "You're the strongest woman I know. But you don't have to do all the things, Sarah. You can let others help. You can let *me* help."

She looked straight into his eyes and something in her chest loosened. A knot that had been held so tight for too long.

"Do you trust me?"

Without hesitation, she responded. "Absolutely."

A small smile crossed his face. "Let me take her. I'll make her wear her floaty and we'll only go as deep as my waist. I won't leave her alone for a second. Not one. And I'll stay right where you can watch, okay?"

Her breath caught in her chest, but still she nodded. It was the right thing to do. "Chest-deep?"

"Chest-deep." He nodded solemnly.

"You won't leave her?"

"Never."

"You won't take your eyes off her?"

"Not for a second."

"You'll keep her safe?" It was the most important question.

"I swear on my life."

His choice of words caused her to wince, but still, she exhaled slowly and nodded a final time. "Okay. Go. Before I change my mind."

Brody didn't jump up right away. Instead, he looked as if

he might kiss her, and in that moment, Sarah wanted nothing more than for him to do it. Instead, he smiled slowly and winked at her before rocking back on his heels and standing up.

"I got you," he said, before jogging down the beach to Rory.

It only took a second before her daughter let out a loud cheer.

She'd done the right thing.

But that didn't make it any easier to watch.

Still, that's exactly what she did.

Sarah didn't take her eyes off Rory and Brody as they made their way to the water's edge. Rory dipped her toe in carefully and let out a small screech at how cold it was. Sarah laughed, but Rory, determined not to back out, moved confidently into the water, her little hand tightly gripped in Brody's.

She'd always loved water. Just like her father. Just because they'd avoided the lake didn't mean they hadn't gone swimming. Sarah had taken her to the town pool for swim lessons when she was younger, and a few times when they'd gone into the city, Sarah always tried to pick a hotel with a pool.

It didn't take long for Rory to forget her hesitation and start splashing the cold water all around. Gradually, the ball of tension in Sarah's gut began to unravel. Brody was so good with Rory. He was laughing and smiling and having just as much fun as the six-year-old. *He really cared about Rory.* It wasn't the first time she'd had that thought. Their relationship was special.

Just like yours.

The thought of it might have made her laugh, if it wasn't true. Her relationship with Brody *was* special.

Her fingers floated to her lips. She could still taste him. Still feel him. It had been such a small kiss that they'd shared, but at the same time, it had been *huge*. With one simple—almost chaste—kiss, her body had come alive in a way it never had before. He was her best friend, yes. *But could he be more? Could things with Brody be different?* Loving him didn't have to mean losing him. *Did it?* Maybe she'd been wrong to keep him at arm's length. *Maybe…*

The stress of the situation and the heat of the day started to take its toll and Sarah's eyes grew heavy as her brain worked through the scenarios of *what if* while she watched her daughter and the man she was falling for play in the water. She leaned back against the tree and gave in to the exhaustion as her eyes drifted shut.

Chapter Seven

IT DIDN'T MATTER that Faith had grown up spending her summers playing in the glacier-fed lake; she still couldn't get used to how cold the water was. Thanks to the heat wave they'd had, the water was actually bearable, even refreshing. And Faith knew that in a few weeks, as the water levels receded a little more, it would warm up even more.

Still, every time her toe slipped from the paddleboard she was lying on and dipped into the water, it startled her.

But the sun was warm, and having paddled a little past the swim line, it was peaceful on the lake, away from all the kids splashing and playing. She rested her head on her arms and let her eyes close. The night before had been a late one. A big wedding of just over two hundred people, with what seemed like two hundred different dietary requests, a drunk mother of the groom, and a party crowd that went well past one in the morning. She needed just a few minutes of sleep.

Or a few hours.

She let the gentle movement of the paddleboard on the waves calm her. As her breath got increasingly slow, Faith allowed her mind to wander. The wedding the night before hadn't only just been a lot of work. It had also been absolutely beautiful. One of the most romantic ceremonies she'd seen. And that meant a lot, because she was undoubtedly the least romantic person in the wedding business, if not in town.

Although, lately, those views seemed to be changing a little bit. Faith hated to admit it, but there was something that tugged at her heartstrings just a little bit when a man and a woman stood in front of all their family and friends and declared their love for each other. And some couples were different. It was just in the way that they looked at each other that you knew they *really* loved each other.

Maybe love could be a thing?

It was a thought she'd been considering more and more. It was impossible not to, really, when all around her, people were coupling up and falling in love. Even Sarah and Brody looked, for all intents and purposes, to be a couple. Faith knew that situation was complicated, but if she didn't know better, she would think that they, too, had finally got over their own bull-shit and were actually dating. She opened her eyes and looked toward the beach long enough to see an intense conversation between Brody and Sarah. She grinned, because it sure looked like he was about to kiss her.

He didn't. She watched Brody go to Rory and lead her into the water. He really was so good to Sarah and her daughter.

Happy for her friend, even if Sarah didn't fully realize what she had in Brody, Faith exhaled slowly and closed her eyes again.

Even if they weren't officially dating, the way Brody cared about Sarah was impressive. It wouldn't be so bad to have a man care about her that way. Not at all.

A deep and completely unexpected wave of sadness washed over her.

Maybe she'd been wrong to keep pushing love away. There'd been more than one man over the years who'd claimed to love her. Had she actually loved them in return, but just hadn't recognized it?

No.

Of that she was certain.

Love was a word people tossed around too easily. It was a word that could hurt. Especially when it was used frivolously. Besides, how did you even know you were in love? She'd been drawn to people before. Attracted. Even intensely attracted. But love?

No.

Right?

No.

No. Definitely not. She'd never been in love. Not even with Noah. He'd been her...*guy friend* in the city before she'd moved officially to Glacier Falls. He'd professed to love her on more than one occasion. And right before she'd moved, he'd started to get a little persistent about their relationship. He'd wanted more, but she'd told him before they'd even started—doing whatever they were doing—that she didn't *do* relationships. Not even a little bit. So it hadn't really been her fault that he'd gotten attached to her.

Breaking things off with him had been for the best. But it had also been hard.

Harder than she'd thought it would be.

Faith let out a deep breath and once more forced the thoughts away.

She was just tired. It had been such a late night and she'd been working so hard that she didn't even know what she was thinking anymore. Faith forced herself to quiet her thoughts and let the warmth of the sun and the gentle rocking of the paddleboard calm her.

It didn't take long before she drifted off into a deep relaxation. That in-between. Where she wasn't quite awake but not quite asleep.

She had no idea how long she'd been lying like that, but it wasn't long enough, when a familiar voice disturbed her peace.

"Hey, beautiful."

Faith's eyes shot open and the paddleboard rocked violently as Logan grabbed the tip and casually wrapped his arms around it to stay afloat. Water dripped from his hair and his eyes twinkled with mischief as he hung off the board.

"Did I disturb you?"

She swallowed hard against her frustration and—although she hated to admit it—the desire that had sparked the moment he appeared. He drove her crazy, that much was certain. But also, he was so damn sexy and the way he looked at her…it was dangerous.

But not nearly as dangerous as entertaining the idea of anything, even a very little something, happening with Logan Langdon.

No way. Of all the men she could entertain such thoughts with, Logan was the worst.

Even if her feelings about love were shifting a little bit, those feelings didn't have any business being connected to Logan.

That would be nothing but trouble.

They'd shared a kiss only a few weeks ago, and just when she'd started to entertain the idea of taking things a little further…Logan couldn't help himself. And he just had to poke at her, the way he always did. Only he'd gone too far shortly after when he'd accused her of being a cold, love 'em and leave 'em type. Maybe it *had* been true. But hearing it come from Logan's lips had pissed her off. And stung a little too much. Especially right when she thought she might be softening toward him.

So much for that.

"You did." She tried to inject as much indifference into her voice as she could, but he only grinned, as if that had been his intention all along. Which, no doubt, it was. "I'm trying to nap."

"Late night?"

"Same as yours."

That wasn't entirely true. She knew for a fact that Logan had a later night than she had. After the wedding party finally wound down, she'd been dead on her feet. There was still so much cleaning up to do, but Logan had sent her back to the house to sleep, insisting that he'd handle the clean-up of anything that couldn't wait. Everything else would be taken care of in the morning. Only, when she'd finally made her way out to the barn, everything had already been done. The chairs had been stacked. The used linens were already in laundry bags and even the dishes had been run through the dishwashers in the kitchen.

He must have been up for hours, doing all that work himself.

"Thank you, by the way," she added after a moment.

"For what?" He winked and then, without warning, dunked under the water. A moment later, Logan reappeared, this time on the side of the paddleboard.

Faith gasped a little at his presence next to her. "Don't scare me like that!" She swatted him and he laughed.

"Come swimming."

"No."

"Come on. It'll be fun."

She shook her head and forced herself to look forward. She could feel his eyes on her, taking in every bare inch of skin that her royal-blue bikini left exposed. Faith wouldn't admit it, not to anyone, but she liked his attentions on her. The knowing that Logan was watching her. Attracted to her. Wanting—

The board shook and tilted dangerously to the side as Logan tried to pull himself up.

"What are you doing?"

"I'm coming to sit with you."

His torso was held out of the water by his thick, muscular arms. It was Faith's turn to check *him* out. And despite herself, she did just that. With her eyes hidden behind her sunglasses, she took in his strong biceps and his chiseled chest muscles that she knew had been honed, not from plenty of gym time but from hard manual labor.

"Like what you see?"

Her mouth dropped open. "You can't see me through my sun—"

"Ah-ha." He winked at her. "You *were* looking at me. I was just guessing."

She blushed and couldn't help but laugh. "Busted," she admitted.

"And?"

"And what?"

"Do you like what you see?"

Faith took the opportunity to take another look. He was still holding himself up effortlessly. "Not bad, I guess," she offered after a moment.

"Not bad?" He jostled the paddleboard again so Faith had to grip the edges.

"I mean it, Logan. I'm not going swimming. It's way too cold."

"What?" His voice was laced with innocence. "But you're so tough," he teased, right as the first cold water drops hit the back of her thigh.

Faith gasped. "Logan! I mean it."

He responded, with another handful of cold water on the back of her leg. But this time, he used his hand to gently, and way too seductively, rub it into her skin. The freezing water instantly turned hot. There was no denying the response his touch elicited in her.

Before she could react properly, he leaned forward on the board, until he was only inches away from her face.

Was he going to kiss her?

Did she want him to?

The answer both confused her and excited her. She reflexively closed her eyes, ready and wanting Logan's lips to meet hers. She let out a small puff of air right as—

The icy water took her breath away as her head submerged. She pushed to the surface, sputtering and coughing. Faith wiped her drenched hair from her face and opened her eyes wide, her sunglasses lost to the lake. "What the hell, Logan?" Faith grabbed at the paddleboard before it floated away, and hung on with one arm.

He was too busy laughing to respond to her, but finally Logan looked at her and his laughter quieted.

He stared at her so intently that it unnerved her.

"What?" she demanded. "What are you staring at?" Self-conscious, Faith wiped at a stray hair on her cheek. "What?" she demanded again.

In a quick, strong kick, Logan moved so he was directly in front of her. "Do you have any idea how incredibly sexy you look right now?" He shook his head and bit his bottom lip. "I mean, I thought that bikini was something, but damn…" He moved closer in the water, and with nowhere to go, Faith was sure he was going to kiss her.

He leaned forward, closed his eyes and—

It was Faith's turn to splash a wave of cold water in his face before she turned, hopped back on the board, and paddled away in the opposite direction. She waited until she was far enough away to let out the breath she'd been holding. Because damn if she hadn't wanted him to kiss her.

Chapter Eight

THE WATER WAS COLD, but Rory didn't seem to mind after she got over the initial shock of it. In fact, Rory loved the water. Brody couldn't help but get caught up in the joy that the little girl got from splashing and kicking and swimming around him in circles. He couldn't remember the last time he'd smiled so wide or laughed so hard.

The fact that Sarah trusted him with her daughter after everything she'd been through wasn't lost on him. It was a big deal. A *very* big deal. He snuck a few glances at her when they'd first gotten in the water, but the last time he'd looked over, it looked as though Sarah had finally relaxed enough to fall asleep.

She trusted him.

That meant everything.

"Having fun, kiddo?"

Rory stopped paddling with her hands and threw them up in the air with a cheer. Water splashed over his face and Brody wiped it with a laugh.

"I'll take that as a yes." He chuckled.

"Wow!" Rory pointed to something over Brody's shoulder. "Can you do that?"

He turned to see what he assumed were Damon's legs straight up in the air. Nearby, Katie laughed and shook her head at her husband's showboating. "Do a handstand under-water?" He turned and asked Rory, who hadn't stopped watching the feet that were now moving in a sort of mime version of walking as Damon showed off. "Totally," Brody said with confidence. He wasn't sure he had the upper body strength that Damon had, and he probably hadn't done a handstand since he was a teenager, but how hard could it be? "No problem."

"Do it!" Rory didn't waste any time in demanding her own performance. "Please," she added with a very strategic lower lip stuck out and a fluttering of her eyelashes. She might be only six, but she definitely had the whole girlish charms thing worked out.

"I don't know, Rory. I promised your mom I wouldn't let you out of my sight." And being underwater would definitely be out of his sight.

"Please!" she pleaded. "It'll only be a second and I'm right here. Nothing will happen. I'm not going anywhere."

Logically, Brody knew all of that was probably true. And it wasn't as if he were going anywhere or being negligent. He'd just pop under the water for a second. No problem. Besides, he could keep his eyes open the whole time. It really wasn't a big deal.

"Okay," he said. "But just for a second." He glanced over at Damon, who now appeared to be doing some sort of synchronized leg dance with his lower half. "And I'm not doing that."

Rory laughed, clearly pleased that she'd gotten her way.

Brody backed up a little bit, and with a big gulp of air, flipped himself forward into the water. It was trickier than he remembered, pulling his legs up straight. Of course, his legs were bigger and heavier than they'd been when he was a kid. But he managed it. And with a flash of pride, he straightened them straight up. Even under the water, he was sure he heard Rory's squeal of pleasure with his performance. He could see her legs kicking beneath the yellow inflatable duck, and because she was so easily pleased, he decided to give her a bit of a show. With all the strength he could muster, Brody began moving his legs in what he hoped looked even half as good as Damon's show.

He couldn't have been under the water more than a few seconds, when he heard Rory squeal again, but this time was different. There was another pair of legs next to hers kicking under her rubber ducky, and in a flash, the remaining air in his lungs rushed out in a burst. He flipped upside down and shot out of the water directly in front of Rory.

And a very angry-looking Sarah.

"Hey." He wiped the water from his face and slicked his hair back. "I was just—"

"You promised." Her voice shook and she clenched her teeth together. She was only barely holding herself back from some sort of outburst. "You promised," she said again. "Brody, you *promised*." She practically spat out the word.

"Promised what?" Confused, he shook his head. "Nothing happened, Sarah. It's all good. Rory and I were—"

"Leaving." She lifted her daughter out of the water and Rory squealed, but not in delight.

"No, Mom! I don't want to go!"

"Sarah." He took a step toward her but the look on her face stopped him. She turned to leave, holding Rory tighter as the little girl struggled in her mom's arms. Brody was vaguely aware that people around them were starting to watch the scene, but he didn't care. "This is crazy. We were just—"

She spun around so quickly, Brody had to take a step back

to keep from falling over. "You left her, Brody! You *left* her." Her voice wavered and Brody could see that she was on the verge of tears and she was desperately trying to hold herself together. "You promised me you wouldn't leave her alone. You *promised.* You told me you wouldn't let her out of your sight, Brody."

"I didn't…I was…" Brody held his arms out at his sides and spun in a half circle, in a desperate attempt to try to explain himself. "Sarah, I—"

"Mom! I want to stay!"

"Don't do this, Sarah." Brody took a step toward her again.

But she pressed her lips together and shook her head once. "You knew what this meant to me, Brody. You *knew.*"

His heart clenched as he felt every beat of the pain and hurt she was feeling. "Sarah," he pleaded. "I'm so—"

"I can't do this." She shook her head to stop him. "Any of it."

This time when she turned to walk away, he didn't try to stop her.

By the time Sarah pulled her car into the driveway, Rory had cried herself to sleep. She dropped her head against the steering wheel and exhaled a long, deep breath.

What the fuck had she just done?

It was a question she'd asked herself at least fifty times on the drive home once Rory had stopped screaming and fallen asleep, allowing her the space to think.

Had she overreacted?

Yes.

Should she have packed up all their stuff and taken off that way?

No.

Was she completely out of her mind?

Oh, hell yes.

Despite being able to logically think it through now, after the fact, Sarah knew she couldn't have done anything different. Something had woken her from her little nap. When she'd opened her eyes after drifting off to sleep, it had taken her a minute to remember where she was, and why she was there. And then when she looked to where she'd last seen Brody and Rory in the lake, she'd only seen Rory in her bright-yellow and purple polka dot bathing suit, the yellow ducky around her waist, it made sense. It had been Rory's screech that had woken her up.

And where was Brody?

He wasn't there.

He was gone.

It all happened so fast after that. She'd never moved so quickly, running down the beach, splashing through the water and grabbing her daughter. It felt as if it took hours to get there, but of course it had only been seconds. And then there was Brody, standing in front of her, water dripping from his hair down his chest, a smile on his handsome face until he realized how upset she was.

Reliving it, Sarah let out a low groan.

She'd totally lost her shit. Everyone had seen it. They must all think she was completely crazy. But then again, maybe not. After all, her husband had died in that lake. The very same lake that she'd just trusted Brody to take her daughter into.

She hit her head a little on the steering wheel. Maybe she'd overreacted. But then again, maybe Brody should have tried harder to make sure she wasn't put in the situation to react at all.

Sarah allowed herself two more deep breaths. When she was feeling at least a little bit calmer, she gathered a still sleeping Rory out of the backseat, leaving everything else for later, and went inside. She avoided looking at Brody's truck that he'd left out front, choosing to ride together to the lake. She'd left him stranded there, but no doubt someone would offer him a ride home. Still, she couldn't help but feel a pang of guilt.

She tucked Rory in, still wearing her now dry bathing suit. The poor thing was exhausted from a day in the sun and crying herself to sleep. Sarah would make it up to her and hopefully she wouldn't be too traumatized from her first visit to the beach.

Sarah poured herself a glass of wine and was just about to sit down on the couch when there was a knock at the door.

She froze and contemplated her options.

She could ignore it. Almost certainly, it was Brody. He'd go away when she didn't answer.

Another knock. This one harder and followed by, "Sarah. Open the door."

Shit.

He wasn't going to go away.

She couldn't risk him waking up Rory. An overtired six-year-old who was already deeply pissed off at her mother for ruining her day at the beach was not going to be fun to deal with.

With a sigh of resignation, Sarah put her glass of wine on the table and moved to answer the door.

Brody stood on her porch, still wearing his swim trunks, now dried, and a T-shirt that she'd never seen before. She realized, belatedly, that she'd probably packed up his things with hers in her haste to get out of there.

He must have seen the question in her eyes. "Logan loaned it to me," he said as way of explanation. "Can I come in?"

She hadn't originally intended to let him in, but still, she found herself pushing the door open before walking back into the living room.

"I'm sorry."

"I'm sorry."

They both said at the same time.

Sarah turned to look at him. He really did look sorry. His face was screwed up in concern and the sadness on his face might have affected her if she wasn't still so angry with him. Because yes, she was sorry for freaking out. But she was still pissed.

"Can I explain?" Brody asked after the moment of silence stretched out between them. "Because I know how it looked, Sarah. I do. I've spent the last few hours going over it and trying to understand how it looked from your point of view. And I get it."

He reached out for her, but she crossed her arms over her chest, unwilling to let him touch her. If he touched her, she knew she would crumble. She knew she would finally be able to see that she *had* been unreasonable and she *had* overreacted. And she would forgive him. And more than anything, at least for the time being, she needed to be mad. Because her anger was the shield she needed to protect her from herself and the thoughts that had been trying to grab hold.

When she didn't answer, Brody started talking. "I know I promised you I wouldn't take my eyes off her, Sarah. And I didn't." She bristled, but he continued. "My eyes were open the whole time underwater." He shook his head. "I know it sounds stupid, considering the circumstances, but I swear to you I was watching her the whole time." He scrubbed his hands over his face, the exhaustion and worry evident all over his handsome features. "She wanted me to do a handstand, and I…well, I know I shouldn't have, but…has she ever asked you for something and you just can't say no?"

He looked so serious and so intensely upset about the prospect of not giving Rory exactly what she wanted right when she asked for it, that Sarah couldn't help herself. She burst out laughing.

"What?" Brody shook his head, confused a moment later when her laughter died down. "How is that funny?"

"Brody." Sarah gained control of herself and once more crossed her arms. "Of course she's asked me for something. Every single day. That's her job as a six-year-old. To push the boundaries and ask for all the things." She shook her head a little. "And it's the parent's job to say no. To not give in to every single thing that she asks for. That's parenting, Brody."

She swallowed hard as the realization of what had just come out of her mouth hit her.

Parenting. Brody.

"Never mind," she added quickly. "I wasn't suggest-ing….well, I wasn't saying…I mean, I know you're not her parent, Brody. You're her friend. Her *coach.*"

It was all too much. Sarah crossed the room and took a big gulp of her wine. She hadn't been trying to imply that Brody had any parenting responsibility or ever would have or anything like that. *Was she?*

She was tired. It had been a long day with too many emotions. She should probably just go to bed before she said something else she regretted.

Sarah put her glass down and started to turn around. Brody needed to leave. "I think you should just—"

Her words died in her throat. Brody stood right in front of her. He was so close she could smell the lingering sunscreen and see the red patch on the tip of his nose where he'd forgotten to reapply it.

"I'm not leaving." His voice was gruff and something flashed in his eyes as he closed the already impossibly small gap between them. "Not before we figure out what is really going on here."

Before she could respond, his arms were around her. His lips were on hers. And nothing else mattered.

It wasn't until the very second that he put his lips on hers that Brody realized how much he'd needed to kiss her again. Her lips on his, her body pressed up against his—it was like an energy force breathing life into his body. From the moment in the lake when she'd looked at him with so much betrayal on her face, grabbed Rory and ran off, he'd felt as though a piece of him had gone with her.

Now...it was back.

Kissing her completed him in a way that both scared and energized him.

He slipped his hands up her back to hold her tighter to him, not willing to let her get away again. He needed to make her see that this was right and good and would not result in anything bad. It couldn't.

Because the way he felt about her was anything but bad. It was so very right.

A small groan escaped her lips, setting off a reaction that threatened to consume him. Every single thing about this woman was absolutely everything to him.

Her hands gripped his back with just as much need as he was feeling, and when Brody moved his kiss to her neck, nibbling and tasting every inch of her sensitive skin, her fingers dug in as her knees buckled beneath his attentions.

He knew he should take things slow with her, that she was emotionally raw. They both were. But there was a very big difference in what his brain was trying to tell him versus what his heart and body were screaming at him.

Brody lifted his lips from her skin long enough to pull her T-shirt over her head. She gasped, and he paused, asking the question with his eyes.

In response, she pulled him close again and kissed him hard, this time with more urgency.

It was the only answer he needed, and when he slipped his hands up to cup her full, luscious breasts through the lace of her bra, she moaned. And when he lowered his mouth to suck her hard, peaked nipple into his mouth, she let out a sound that could only be described as ecstasy.

How long had it been since she'd been touched like this? Ever?

Brody remembered the confession she'd made to him about her marriage. *Had Sarah ever felt the touch of a man who couldn't get enough of her? Who thought she was the sexiest woman alive?*

Damn.

She deserved this. She deserved so much more. And he wanted to give it all to her.

He cupped and squeezed gently as he kissed and licked first one nipple, and then the other. Sarah threaded her fingers through his hair, urging him on. It was a call he was more than happy to answer. But he needed more.

When he moved to unclasp her bra, she froze.

Brody lifted his head and looked her in the eye. "Sarah?"

"It's just..."

"We don't have—"

"No!" She swallowed hard and her lips curled up into a shy smile. "It's just...it's..."

"It's okay." He kissed her gently and once again moved his hands to unclasp her bra. This time she didn't protest, and he slipped the lacy garment from her arms, leaving her exposed in front of him.

He sucked in a sharp breath as he took her in. She was gorgeous. Curvy and soft and absolutely perfect.

He took his time taking her all in, enjoying the moment he'd waited so long for. Finally, he brought his gaze up to meet hers. She looked scared and unsure. "You," he said slowly, his voice low and full of need, "are absolutely gorgeous."

"I'm—"

"Perfect."

Finally, Sarah's lips curled up into a smile as she reached out and tugged at the shirt he wore.

Brody readily complied and in a flash, his shirt was on the floor and his lips were back on hers.

Skin on skin, everything felt more intense, including the need building inside him. He had to have her. And judging by the way she was kissing him back, she needed him just as badly. *But...*

"Wait." He pulled back, without releasing his grip on her. "What about...Rory..." He jerked his head toward the hallway. "I know she—"

"Is fast asleep." Sarah's words came out on a breath. "She was so tired. She won't be waking up anytime soon."

It was all he needed to hear. He pressed his lips back on hers and kissed her with a hunger that was only barely contained.

He backed her up until they were in front of the couch. He moved to the button of her cut-off shorts and hesitated. He needed to be sure. With everything between them, he couldn't risk moving too fast or doing anything she wasn't one hundred percent on board with.

"Sarah?"

She looked at him with heavily lidded eyes full of need.

"Do you want this?"

Her response was to take a half step back so she had space to unbutton her own shorts and slide them, along with her panties, to the floor.

She stood before him, completely naked, and it took every single ounce of self-control that he could muster to keep from jumping on her. Never in his life had he seen such a gorgeous woman and she was here, in front of him, offering herself to him.

He shed himself of his swim trunks, his own need strong and proud standing at attention between his legs.

Brody swallowed hard and counted to three in his head before reaching for her.

Sarah closed her eyes as he cupped her cheek with his hand. She leaned into his touch as he stroked a gentle circle on the soft skin, before slowly sliding his hand down the length of her. When he reached her waist, he pulled her to him and kissed her again. This time with nothing between them.

It was his turn to moan when he felt her, wet with desire against him.

As gently as he could, Brody backed her up until Sarah was lying on the couch with him hovering over her. Her legs spread, and his throbbing cock pressed up against her entrance when he stopped.

Shit.

He didn't have a condom.

Reading his mind, Sarah reached around him and pressed him toward her. "It's okay," she murmured. "I'm on the Pill."

He didn't question it as his body and the need raging through him took over. He was looking directly into her deep eyes as he finally slid inside her, so he didn't miss the flash of passion reflected back at him. And he also didn't miss the tear that slipped down her cheek moments later as her orgasm crested, and she cried out her release.

Chapter Nine

SHE WAS AT THE LAKE. The wind blew her hair off her face because it was cold. Not quite summer yet, but a beautiful spring day and they'd gone to the beach for a picnic.

Sarah turned to see Josh where she'd left him on the blanket with the baby while she went for a short walk. She'd told him she was looking for crocuses, but in truth, she'd needed a minute alone. Because she knew if she sat there with him, playing happy family for even one more second, she thought she might burst. And that wasn't fair.

Nothing felt fair anymore.

Especially not the conversation she was about to have with her husband. That, more than anything else, didn't feel fair to anyone.

"Hey!" Josh looked up from the blanket where he was lying on his side, propped up on one elbow, dangling a toy over their infant daughter. "How was your walk? Did you find any crocuses? They were your mom's favorite, weren't they?"

A pang of guilt hit her in the chest. *He knew what her mother's favorite flower had been.* Even though she'd died when Sarah herself was only a toddler, her husband knew what her favorite flower had been.

That was love.

She forced a smile and shook her head. "No," she said. "No crocuses."

"Too bad." Josh sat up. "Come sit. Let's have those strudels I brought from Sweetie Pies. I know the cherry is your favorite."

More guilt.

Of course he knew what her favorite dessert was. They'd been together since they were seventeen. They knew everything about each other. They were best friends.

Best friends.

And that was the problem.

With a sigh, Sarah settled across from her husband on the blanket and crossed her legs. "We need to talk."

His handsome face changed in an instant. The topic of conversation couldn't have been a surprise; she'd brought it up more than once in the last few months. But each time she mentioned it, Josh changed the subject or made light of it and laughed it off. But Sarah wouldn't let him do that today. She couldn't. Because every day that went by that they didn't talk, she was growing more and more unhappy.

"Now is not the time." Josh crossed his arms. "We're having a good day, Sarah. Don't ruin it with this nonsense."

"It's not nonsense, Josh. It's..." Her head dropped to her chest. She knew she was doing the right thing. She knew it in her heart. They both deserved so much more than to live the rest of their lives in a deep friendship with their partner and nothing else. They deserved a spark. Some passion...*something.*

"You know how much I love you, Josh," she tried again. "You are my best friend."

"Then why are you doing this, Sarah?" He shook his head, as if he could stop himself from hearing what she had to say by force of will. "You love me and I love you and we have this beautiful little girl and—"

"It's not enough."

He froze. His eyes narrowed and he shook his head with a grunt. "Not enough?" Josh waved his arms around. "How is this not enough for you, Sarah? We have it all. Do you know how many couples would kill for what we have? No, we're not making out like teenagers or having sex in the kitchen," he continued. "We're parents, Sarah. We have responsibilities."

"We never made out like teenagers, Josh." She could feel the color rising to her cheeks. She wouldn't back down this time. She couldn't. She'd made her decision and she was going to stick with it. It was for the best, and Josh would come to see it too; she knew he would. In time. "Not even when we *were* teenagers. We haven't had sex since Rory was born," she added. "And even before she was born…I can't actually remember the last time. Maybe when we conceived her. And even then, it was…"

She trailed away. There was no point in going down that road. Not again. Because the truth was, they both knew that their sex life was terrible. It always had been. When they were young and inexperienced, they'd both just assumed that was how it was done and that it would get better as they got older. But it didn't. The few times they did have it, it was mechanical and it felt forced, as if it were something that they were *expected* to do. Not something they *wanted* to do.

"We deserve better, Josh. We both do."

On the blanket, Rory gurgled and kicked her legs. She was such a happy baby. Sarah couldn't help but smile whenever she looked at her. But this time her smile was also full of pain.

She looked up at Josh again. "That's why I want a divorce."

She watched as, in front of her eyes, something inside Josh

broke. His face crumpled and his shoulders fell as he stared down into the blanket for a long time.

When he finally looked up, something in his eyes had shifted. The light was gone. It changed his entire face into someone she didn't recognize. It scared her.

"We don't get divorces, Sarah. My family doesn't *do* divorce. No one has ever had one. I'm not going to be the first." He got to his feet and paced away from the blanket to the edge of the trees. Sarah jumped to her feet, too, but then he turned and walked back to her. He looked down at their baby. "What about Rory?" he finally asked, his voice soft. "To grow up in a broken home? That's not what we wanted for her, Sarah. It's not fair to her."

"Josh, it's not fair to Rory to teach her that it's okay to settle for less than what you deserve." She reached for him but he shook her off. "We will still be amazing parents. We can do this together. And we can also each find the love we deserve. You know that's true, Josh. You *know* it." She pleaded with her eyes for him to admit what they both knew. She knew in her heart that Josh agreed with her. She just *knew* it.

For a moment, she believed he would agree with her.

He nodded and then shook his head violently. "It doesn't matter what I know," he said after a moment. "We made this decision together, Sarah, and now we need to see it through."

Her heart fell. It was going to be harder for him to admit the truth than she'd thought. She wasn't a crier, but now tears of frustration and hurt and sadness for everything they'd never had spilled unchecked down her cheeks. "Josh." His name was barely a whisper on her breath. "Please don't make this harder than it has to be."

Tears slipped from her husband's eyes now and the sight of it almost broke her. "I love you, Sarah." He nodded, as if he'd made up his mind about something. She tried to take a step toward him, but he stepped backward. "No." He held out a hand to stop her. "I need a minute."

"Josh, I—"

"I'm going for a swim."

"A swim?"

No.

She couldn't let him go. It was too cold. He was in no state. Josh turned and jogged down from the grassy picnic area toward the lake. He pulled his shirt off as he went. Sarah glanced toward the baby still content on the blanket and back to Josh. She couldn't leave Rory.

"Shit."

Quickly, she grabbed up the baby and started running as well as she could with Rory held tight to her chest. "Josh!" She screamed his name as he dove into the lake and started swimming away from her. "Josh!" She screamed again and again, squeezing the baby tighter to her chest.

He needed to come back. It couldn't end this way. He needed to turn around. He *had* to.

"Sarah!"

Josh?

She couldn't see through her tears and her panic. But he was calling her.

"Sarah!"

Where was he? She couldn't see him. She shook her head back and forth, desperate to find him, but she couldn't see anything but blackness.

I'm here! She tried to yell, but no sound came out. *Josh. I'm here.*

Tears poured from her eyes. A sob choked in her throat.

"Sarah!" His hands were on her. *He was there.* He was with her. "Open your eyes, Sarah! Wake up."

She sat up with a start, her eyes flying open and her heart

racing. "Josh?" She spun around as her eyes slowly focused on the man before her.

A man who was not her husband.

Because her husband was dead.

He'd gone for a swim and never came back. Reality crushed her like a weight as the dream faded away.

It was Brody who'd been calling her name. Brody with his arms around her. Brody who she'd fallen asleep on the couch with after—

"Mommy?"

Rory?

Rory!

Instantly, Sarah's mother instincts kicked in. Fortunately, Brody—whose presence she was still trying to reconcile in her head...never mind the fact that they were naked or that they'd had sex; she'd deal with that later—had already jumped into action. He tossed some clothes in her direction. She tugged the shorts on over her hips and was just pulling the T-shirt—which she realized belatedly was his—over her head when Rory came into the room.

"Mom?" The way that Rory rubbed at her eyes, still half asleep and with her stuffed rabbit, Bramble, tucked into the crook of her arm and still wearing her bright bathing suit, her little girl looked even younger. "What's wrong?"

Sarah glanced around, hoping that Brody had disappeared. He had, and she breathed a sigh of relief as she crossed the room to her daughter. "Nothing's wrong, kiddo. Did you have a bad dream?"

"I heard you screaming."

Screaming? Shit.

Her dream.

She was still vibrating from the images she'd seen in her head. It had been so real. All of it. Like it had just happened moments ago, and not almost six years ago.

Sarah took a deep breath and knelt next to Rory. "You know how sometimes you have a bad dream?" Rory nodded. "Well, that's what I had. Just a bad dream, and I must have screamed out loud. I'm sorry I scared you."

She stroked her daughter's hair and pulled her close.

Sarah couldn't be sure who was doing the comforting in that moment. Holding her little girl was a soothing balm to the ache in her chest.

After a few minutes, Rory giggled and pulled away from her. "You smell like Brody."

Sarah froze, her breath caught in her throat. "Brody?"

"You're wearing his shirt, silly."

Sarah almost corrected Rory that it was Logan's shirt, and Brody had only been wearing it, but it definitely wasn't a detail that mattered. Instead, she said, "Let's get you back to bed. It's late."

"You should go to bed, too. Don't sleep on the couch, Mom. It's not very comfy."

Sarah couldn't help but smile at how observant her daughter was, which was also incredibly worrisome. She'd only been seconds away from Rory discovering her with Brody on the couch where they'd—she couldn't think about it. At least not yet.

Rory was exhausted, and fortunately crawled back into her bed with no complaint, her eyes closing almost as soon as her head hit the pillow. Sarah sat and watched her chest rise and fall for what felt like hours before finally slipping from Rory's bedroom.

She was only a little bit surprised when she found Brody sitting in the kitchen, a cup of tea in front of him, and an extra steaming mug set out for her. "I assumed you would have left," she said.

"I didn't really know what…well…it didn't seem…"

"You should go."

"Don't you think we should talk about it?"

Sarah turned from the sink where she'd been staring at the dirty dishes. "About what?"

That they'd made love on her living room couch.

That he'd made her feel in a way she'd never experienced before.

That Rory almost caught them together naked in the living room.

That she'd felt so safe in his arms she'd fallen asleep.

That she'd dreamed in detail about her last conversation with her husband.

That she'd woken up screaming his name.

There was more than one thing that they could talk about. And she wasn't interested in discussing any of them. Before he could answer, Sarah shook her head. "No. You should go."

Brody pushed up from the kitchen table and crossed the room to her. "Sarah, I don't think I should leave you."

"I'm fine." It was a lie of the worst kind, because she was anything but fine. "It was a mistake." Another lie. But this one could at least protect both of them from making the situation worse. "We shouldn't have done that."

"You don't believe that."

She squeezed her eyes shut to keep from looking at him. But when she closed her eyes, all she could see was the broken expression on Josh's face moments before he'd run into the lake. A sob caught in her throat. "Brody, I can't do this. I told you before that we need to be friends. I can't…I just can't do this. Today was too much."

Had that been what the dream was about? Was Josh trying to tell her no? She'd ruined one man she'd loved. She wouldn't do it again. And there was Rory to think about, too.

She still couldn't look at him, but when he placed his hand

on her hip and pulled her closer, for a second she considered giving in to his touch. Her entire body yearned to let him hold her. But that would take them down a dangerous path again. The last time he'd held her, he'd kissed her and then... *no*.

She shook her head. It was going to be too hard. She couldn't do this. There was only one way to protect them both.

Sarah swallowed hard and with a deep breath, forced herself to step back while at the same time, pushing him away. "Leave." Her voice cracked on the word, so she tried again, this time with more force. "Leave, Brody." She swallowed back tears. "I need you to leave. We can't do this. It was a mistake and yes," she added before he could object, "I *do* believe that. I never should have even let you in. You betrayed me."

She steeled herself against the look of disbelief and pain on his face while she spoke. A little bit of hurt in the short term would protect them all. It was worth it.

"Sarah, this doesn't—"

"Let me talk." She interrupted him. "I trusted you with the most important person in my life. You made me a promise, and you couldn't keep it." It was ridiculous and shaky ground, she knew, but it was all she had to stand on. Sarah forced herself not to look away when she delivered her final blow. "You're not the man I thought you were." She saw him wince, but still continued. "And I was wrong. About everything. I'm sorry if I gave you the wrong idea tonight, but it was a mistake. A terrible mistake. You need to leave."

She held her ground despite the fact that she was sure her legs would give out on her at any moment.

He looked as though he were going to say something, and she didn't know whether she'd be able to handle it if he did. Finally, mercifully, he nodded. "If that's what you really want."

She nodded curtly. "It is." *A lie. A terrible, horrible lie.* Her eyes burned with unshed tears, but she willed herself not to cry.

"Okay. I'll go."

She clenched her hands into tight fists to keep herself from reaching out as he walked away from her, wearing nothing but his swim trunks. The moment she heard the front door click shut, she released her hands and let her head drop to her chest with a long exhale. She no longer had the energy to cry as she made her way to bed, wondering whether she'd just made the biggest mistake of her life.

Chapter Ten

IT HAD BEEN two days since they'd been at the lake. Two days since Faith allowed herself to entertain, even for one second, the idea of opening herself up to a relationship.

With Logan.

No.

She pushed that thought out of her head for at least the millionth time since Sunday. A relationship? That was one thing. Maybe, *maybe* she could let herself entertain the idea of such a thing. One day. With the right man.

But the right man was definitely *not* Logan Langdon.

No way.

Which was why it was maddening that he kept creeping into her thoughts. All. Of. The. Time.

It didn't help that they worked together every day, all day in the barn setting up and preparing for the next big wedding event. She couldn't think with him around. Even when he wasn't talking to her, or teasing her, he was…there. He was watching her. Or maybe he wasn't. But it sure felt like he was.

And she couldn't think properly that way. She needed space.

Which was why she'd made an excuse to slip into town to finalize her ad campaign plans. She still hadn't told Hope about what she was thinking of and she didn't plan to. Not until it was well underway. And hopefully successful. Hope and Levi were due to be home in a few months so they could monitor the later stages of the pregnancy carefully with Hope's doctor. The last thing they were going to want to worry about upon returning home was keeping up with the bookings at Ever After. If this marketing strategy was successful, Faith would be able to keep the ranch fully booked up, even through the winter months, which would be a huge stress relief for her sister.

And her.

She hated to admit it. But more and more, Faith was actually starting to enjoy the business of planning and executing happy-ever-afters for couples. It made her feel good in a way that she couldn't begin to describe, deep in her soul. And every time she heard the words, "I do," it was as if something inside her rearranged a little to make space for love.

Was that why Hope had loved this business? Because of the way it made her feel inside?

Hope had always been the romantic twin. The one who believed in forever. But that was only because it had been Faith who'd discovered the truth about their parents, not Hope. And she'd never tell her twin sister about the day that she'd overheard her parents arguing. She'd crept down the stairs and eavesdropped as her mom cried and her dad said terrible things that only made her mom cry harder before she, too, started saying things that made her father wince in pain.

She couldn't hear all of what they were saying, but the little she did hear had changed everything. She could see it on their faces, the pain they were causing each other with every word spoken. The scene had hardened something inside Faith that day.

How could the two people who professed to love each other more than anyone else in the whole world hurt each other in such a way? Faith was only fifteen, but it was easy to see then that only the person who you let into your heart and loved the most could ever have the power to hurt you in such ways.

If that was love, she didn't want a damn thing to do with it. Even worse to Faith was the fact that they pretended to love each other deeply when in reality they were just like everyone else, just as capable of hurting the one they loved the most in the worst possible ways. With such hurtful words. All because of a terrible secret that had finally come out.

And just like that, Faith made the decision to keep love away. It wasn't worth it. Opening herself up to that kind of pain? No thanks.

It had been many years ago, and despite the fact that she had never again witnessed anything like that between her parents again, it had stuck with her and the vision of the scene had clouded everything else. Her young teenage brain had completely changed her idea of love in an instant. With a sigh, Faith shook her head in an effort to clear her head.

Had she gotten it wrong?

It wasn't a thought she'd ever had before, but she wasn't too proud to consider it.

Maybe she'd gotten it wrong all these years?

Faith cleared her throat and packed up her things from the little table in the corner of Sweetie Pies. She needed some air to think.

The idea that she could have been wrong about something that had been so influential in shaping her entire adult life had shaken her. The moment she was outside, Faith closed her eyes, took a deep breath, and filled her lungs with the heavy air and the sweet smells of summer.

She counted to three and opened her eyes, just in time to see Brody Morris waving at her while he crossed the street.

"Hey," he said when he got close enough. "Just the person I wanted to see."

"Oh yeah? Why's that?" Faith opened her arms to greet Brody with a quick hug. He'd quickly become a good friend since he'd been in Glacier Falls. It was always good to see him, but at that moment, she particularly welcomed the distraction from her own thoughts.

"I had a proposition for you."

She wiggled her eyebrows and burst out laughing. It was no secret that it wouldn't be her who Brody was making any kind of proposition to. She bit back the urge to ask him about Sarah and what had happened after their blow-out at the lake.

He blushed and shook his head before continuing. "I've catered a few weddings for you, now."

"You have," she said. "And the food always gets rave reviews."

"Of course it does." He laughed. "Which is why I want to cater more."

"More?"

Brody nodded. "And by more, I mean *all*."

"You want to cater *all* of the weddings at Ever After Ranch?" She'd be lying if she said it wasn't a surprise. Taking on the catering for all of her events would be a ton of work, which was why she'd always used a variety of vendors to spread the work around. The last thing they wanted to do was burn out a caterer and risk future events.

"I do." He nodded and then laughed at the realization of what he'd said. "I mean, we can work out a deal. If you give me an exclusive contract, I'd be able to offer you a discount and…"

"It would benefit both of us," she finished for him.

"Absolutely." He grinned. "Do we have a deal?"

This was the kind of decision that Hope would have made, but Hope wasn't around and she'd left Faith in charge, which theoretically meant that she trusted her. "Let's sit down next week and work out the details," she said. "But I don't see why not. If you have the capacity for it, it could be a perfect relationship."

"Happily ever after, right?" He laughed and his eyes lit up, giving Faith an idea that she hoped he would agree to.

"But there's just one more thing..."

Chapter Eleven

"YOU SAID I'D DO WHAT?"

Brody hadn't been sure how Amy would take the news, but he'd agreed to it as part of the deal with Faith, so he needed to make her okay with the fact that he'd signed her up to be part of a photo shoot for Faith's upcoming ad campaign.

"It's just a few pictures." He tried not to make it sound like a big deal, but when Faith had asked him to be a *groom* in the shoot, and supply his own *bride*, he really hadn't known who else to ask. Obviously Faith would have assumed that he'd ask Sarah, and of course that's who he'd want next to him in a white gown, pretending to be his blushing bride—or in real life maybe one day—but she wasn't talking to him.

It had been two days since they'd…well, since the lake and their subsequent activities at her house. He didn't know how to think of it. At the time, it had been perfect. Better than perfect. Being with Sarah had just felt right. Better than anything he'd ever experienced.

And when she'd fallen asleep with her head on his chest, he'd lain awake, stroking her hair and taking in every second of his time with her. All Brody had been able to think about was how going forward, everything would be different between them. They could finally be together, and he could give her everything she'd ever deserved. But then there'd been the nightmare, with her screaming out Josh's name and the subsequent chaos when she'd kicked him out and then…nothing.

Sarah had effectively ghosted him, as if they hadn't shared the most intense night together. As if she hadn't felt the things with him that he *knew* she'd felt. He knew it. So, yes. He would have liked to have asked Sarah to be his bride in the photo shoot, but that wasn't going to happen. Which was why he needed Amy to agree.

"You're kidding, right?" His head chef leaned against the counter and rolled her eyes. "You know I'm not into you."

He had to shake his head. "It's not real."

"I got that."

"Please, Amy. I know it's not in your job description or anything, but I promised her that I'd help and she gave me the contract. We're going to be doing all of the Ever After weddings."

That got her attention. "*All* the weddings?"

He nodded. "All of them." Brody couldn't help the smile that crossed his face. Getting the extra catering events would be challenging, for sure—he might even need to hire on some part-time help—but it would be huge when it came to cash flow. Especially considering the day before, Amy had informed him that she couldn't get all the burners on the stove to light. Which would mean yet another service call from Al the appliance guy, which would mean another, bigger dip into his savings. The extra catering gigs would help, but he still needed to come up with a bit more cash to give him some breathing room.

Because if he couldn't make a go of this restaurant, he would be in trouble. Real trouble. Brody didn't even want to think about what that would look like, but it might mean leaving Glacier Falls—and Sarah—for good. And even if she currently wasn't speaking to him, that wasn't a risk he was willing to take.

"Okay," Amy said after a few minutes.

"Okay?"

"Okay, I'll do it. I'll take the stupid pictures."

Brody didn't bother trying to hide his smile.

"But I'm not doing them with you. You're totally not my type."

"Awesome, Amy. Thanks." He did a double take as Amy's words caught up with him. "Wait." He turned to look at her. "What do you mean?"

"About not being my type? I didn't think I had to explain that one to you." A slow, sly grin crossed her face and she crossed her arms over her chest. "I want to do the pictures with Nicole."

"Nicole?"

She nodded slowly and, for a second, her smile faded. "I know you said Faith wanted a couple, and I'll work it out and find someone to be your bride," Amy said quickly. "But I really think that this will be…well, you don't think that will be a problem, do you? I mean…I know that's not really what she asked for but—"

"I actually think it's a great idea," Brody answered honestly. "And I have a feeling that Faith will feel exactly the same way." It was the truth, and seeing his head chef's face light up with the idea of it, gave him hope. After all, love was love; no matter what it looked like, it felt the same and it was incredible and needed to be celebrated.

Which was why he needed to get through to Sarah. Because with each passing moment, everything became clearer —he was desperately in love with her and more than anything, he needed her to understand that and see it too.

It had been a long day and by the time Sarah saw the last patient out of the office and locked up behind Doctor Friesen, she was dead on her feet. All she wanted to do was go home, kick up her feet, and forget about...well, everything.

Especially Brody.

It had been two days, and it still made her cringe to think about everything that had happened.

And what she'd done.

How could she have slept with Brody? All she'd done was make a complicated mess of everything. More complicated than it already was. And it already was.

Sleeping with him. Feeling his hands on her skin. His lips on her. His body making love to her body...it had been...*perfect.*

Sarah hated to admit it, but it was true. If she closed her eyes, she could still feel him inside her, making her feel things that she had never felt before. *Never.*

But then she could remember the rest, too. The dream. *Nightmare.* And the subsequent reality of everything.

No.

None of that had been perfect. Far from it. She'd screwed up, and for the life of her, Sarah had no idea how she was ever going to face him again. She'd been doing a good job of ignoring him and his text messages so far, but that couldn't go on forever. Especially with the soccer game in Cedar Springs and wind-up party on Sunday.

Shit. The wind-up party.

With everything going on, she'd completely forgotten.

Sarah leaned back against the building and dropped her head. She'd completely spaced on the party and after she'd made such a big deal about it to Audrey Hill, she'd never live it down.

Not that she cared.

Not really.

But even if she didn't care, the kids deserved a celebration and there was only one way they were going to get one at this point. The game and party were meant to be on Sunday, and even if she had the time—which she didn't because she'd promised Nicole she'd help out with some sort of project she needed her for on Friday night—she'd never pull off the party in four days.

There was only one thing to do. Sarah pulled her cell phone from her purse, ignored the unread text messages from Brody, and scrolled down, to another series of unread texts—from Audrey.

Hi there. Can I help with anything?

Any info on the party?

Need any help, Sarah?

Haven't heard anything…

Sarah groaned. Brody hadn't been the only one she was avoiding. Although maybe if she'd actually opened any of Audrey's texts, Sarah might have remembered the party earlier. No help for it now.

She hated to do it, but Sarah moved her fingers across the screen and quickly typed out a message to her rival.

• • •

So sorry. Something has come up and I just haven't had time to organize anything for the kids. Do you have any time this week?

Sarah held her breath and sent the message. Seconds later, the reply came in.

No problem at all!! I have a great idea. You just take care of yourself.

She rolled her eyes and tucked the phone away. If she wasn't so relieved to have something off her plate, she might have given a shit about the passive-aggressiveness of Audrey's reply.

But she just couldn't find it in herself to care.

After spending the afternoon in his office working out some more catering menu options and a new price list for Faith, Brody needed to stretch his legs. Thankfully, Sweetie Pies was right down the street. A fresh baked muffin and an iced coffee would be the perfect reward for coming up with a whole new catering plan so quickly. After Faith had agreed—with her photography stipulation—there was no way Brody was going to risk her changing her mind, so he'd gotten right to work.

He'd also had a bit of time to crunch the numbers. The extra catering would be a huge revenue influx, and it would help, but things would still be a little tight. He'd planned so carefully before buying the restaurant. He had money set aside for the renovations and a savings account in case things didn't go according to his detailed business plan. But still. There'd been too much he hadn't planned for.

Brody couldn't remember the last time he'd felt so defeated.

If one more thing went sideways, he could be in trouble. He'd need to come up with something else.

A few minutes later, his treats in hand, Brody headed toward the park in the middle of Main Street. He needed the space to think and roll through some options in his head before returning to Birchwood.

He stopped short before crossing the street to the park, and looked instead to the Hub. There was a brand-new business that was definitely thriving. Of course, it probably didn't hurt that a billionaire had funded the start-up. Even allowing himself to entertain the thought made Brody feel bad. Because everyone knew it wasn't the funding from her mega-rich husband that was making the Hub a booming success. It was all Katie: her planning, her business model, and the atmosphere she'd created there.

Still, maybe he needed to find himself a billionaire. He shook his head with a laugh. No way. He didn't need an investor. He'd figure it out. But still, the idea of spending a few minutes surrounded by his successful friends suddenly sounded a lot more appealing than sitting alone.

"Hey, Brody."

The moment he walked through the door, Katie waved at him from across the room where she was stacking piles of books. He moved across the room toward her and glanced down at the hiking guides she was arranging.

"Can I help you find something today? Or were you looking at renting a bike again?"

He had definitely been enjoying mountain biking and exploring the trails around town. So much so that he was starting to think about buying his own bike instead of constantly renting them. Not that he had the cash flow at the moment. But hopefully soon.

"I was hoping that some of your good business juju vibes would rub off on me, actually." Something about her kind face and easy smile made him open up. Besides, she'd just recently graduated with a business degree; if anyone would have some advice, it very well could be her.

Her brow furrowed and her smile faded. "Uh-oh. Don't tell me Birchwood is in trouble. I absolutely love eating there."

Trouble? There was definitely some trouble.

"Well, not trouble so much. At least not yet. But if things don't start going in the opposite direction, meaning more money in than out, there will absolutely be some trouble."

He'd had no intention of airing his issues when he'd walked into the shop, but once he started talking, he couldn't seem to stop. A few minutes later, and he'd told Katie all about the broken air conditioner and stove.

"I need a really solid summer season, or I'll be looking for an investor or a For Sale sign."

With a book still in her hand, Katie reached out and squeezed his arm. "I know it's hard, Brody. A new business is never easy. And I'm so sorry you're having so many start-up issues. You know, an investor might not be a bad idea." She shrugged as she said it. "It's probably not what you want to hear, but sometimes it's okay to play to your strengths and bring in someone else to benefit from their strengths."

"Like their money?" He laughed. That was a strength he could absolutely get behind.

Katie smiled. "Yes, money. But also business experience." She looked very serious as she spoke. "I know I had an investor who made things easy," she said, as if she'd read his mind. "But I also spent a lot of time learning and studying about business. And I don't know yet if the Hub will be the success I hope it will be, but the business stuff? It's a bit of a strength." She shrugged and the seriousness on her face vanished, replaced once again by a big smile. "I don't know," she said. "It's just a thought. And it could be an option for you. Damon's buddy Nick is still in town, and he's been thinking about getting involved in the economy here. Says it's a good invest-ment." She winked. "And he's right. Glacier Falls is a town on the rise. Besides, Nick definitely has more money than he knows what to do with. It would do him some good to channel it into something productive." She laughed.

Brody shook his head. He'd only met Nick a few times. Together, Nick and Damon had developed some sort of computer chip and sold it for a ridiculous sum of money a few years back. Nick had come out for Damon and Katie's wedding celebration a few weeks ago and had never left. There was some speculation that it wasn't just the town's potential keeping him around, but also a certain blonde wedding planner who had caught his interest. Not that Faith was inter-ested. Everyone could see that there was something between her and Logan, even if they couldn't or wouldn't see it themselves.

"I'll keep it in mind," Brody said, despite the fact that he had no intention of taking on an investor. But he did feel a little bit better after just talking to her for a few minutes. "Thanks, Katie. I appreciate the chat."

"Any time." She gestured to the muffin still in his hand. "Is that one of Sweetie Pies' lemon poppyseed muffins? They're so good. I was thinking of talking to them about putting together some goodie bags for my customers who want to go out on a day trip. Like a few snacks that they can enjoy on the trail."

"Just snacks?"

Katie shrugged. "Sandwiches would be good, too. But they only do baked goods and—"

"I can do sandwiches." The idea came so swiftly that it almost took Brody off guard. "And trail mix and even some freshly baked granola bars. Maybe even a little pasta salad or... I have a million packable lunch ideas."

Katie nodded as he spoke. "I didn't even think of Birch-wood, Brody. I can't believe I didn't, but...a gourmet lunch is absolutely something my clients would enjoy. If you can cut me some kind of deal…"

"And I could include an 'adventure wind-down' dinner coupon for later that night."

"Yes! No one wants to cook after a big day out, especially vacationers." She laughed. "Brody, this is a great idea."

He absolutely had to agree. It was a *much* better idea than looking for an investor, and it might just be the little bit of extra income he needed to keep things going in the right direction. Over the next few minutes while they bashed out some more details, Brody was even happier that he'd stopped in to the Hub. There was definitely some good juju rubbing off. Now, if he could just keep that going, he might actually have some luck getting through to Sarah.

Chapter Twelve

"HEY, KIDDO." Sarah's dad greeted her with a hug when she arrived to pick up Rory. "Did you have an okay day?"

She tried to nod, but couldn't even muster up the energy to lie to her dad. Instead, she offered him a lame shrug. "It was... well...let's just say that I'm looking forward to today being over."

Ed nodded knowingly and pressed his lips together. "I thought it might be a hard day for you today."

Sarah stopped short as she walked into the kitchen, where Rory was coloring at the table. *Why would her dad think today would be hard? There was no way he could know about Brody and...*

She swallowed hard and gave Rory a kiss on the top of her head. For the next few minutes, she let her daughter tell her all about her day and what she'd been up to with her grandfather. But even while she listened to Rory recount their adventures in staining the deck and picking blackberries down by the river, Sarah couldn't shake off her dad's comment.

Finally, when Rory excused herself to go out to the yard to kick her soccer ball, Sarah looked across the table to her dad. "Why did you think today would be hard?"

The look he gave her was full of fatherly concern. "It's July 12," he said softly. When she didn't immediately react, he added, "Sarah, today is your—"

"Wedding anniversary." She dropped her chin to her chest as everything made sense. The heaviness she'd been feeling all day. It had been more than the stress of everything that had happened with Brody. Of course it had been more.

Oh God.

How could she have forgotten?

She shook her head gently and looked up. "I totally forgot. Well," she added quickly at the look on her dad's face, "I didn't forget *forget*. But it explains a lot about why I'm feeling so off today, I think."

Ed nodded gently. "Kiddo, I still feel it on your mother's and mine anniversary. It's been a long, long time, but I can still remember that day like it was yesterday. Standing next to the love of my life and promising forever was the best day of my life. I'll cherish it always."

Sarah watched her dad carefully. "Why didn't you ever date after she died, Dad?"

The question was unexpected for both of them. She hadn't any intention of ever asking him about his love life. They weren't close like that. But it suddenly seemed important.

Across the table, Ed took a deep breath and let it out slowly before continuing. "Honestly?"

"Of course."

"I was satisfied."

It wasn't the answer she'd expected. Sarah tilted her head in question. "Satisfied?"

His face softened while he spoke. "With your mother, I'd experienced my greatest love. I knew I had been loved so deeply and so completely by her that I'd never be able to find anything that came close. Anything else would be second best, and I didn't want anything that wasn't everything. Does that make sense?"

It did. But not for the reasons her dad would have expected. "I think so…"

"I expected as much." He grinned. "It was the same for you and Josh."

The comment took her off guard. Instinctively, she shook her head.

"I understand," he continued. "That's why you've never wanted to—"

"No." She stopped him.

"No?"

Guilt and confusion flooded through her. She was a strong woman. A woman who didn't allow herself to give in to emotions. But when it came to this issue, she was a complete and total mess, and it was starting to piss her off. "Josh and I didn't have the same thing that you and Mom did, Dad." She shook her head as he started to speak again. "Don't get me wrong, I loved Josh very much. But it wasn't the complete and totally consuming type of love that you and Mom shared. We never had that."

He opened his mouth to say something, but closed it again as Sarah came to a decision of her own.

"You know what, Dad? Would you mind Rory hanging out here a bit longer? I think there's something I need to do."

He nodded and blinked hard, but not before Sarah saw the glisten of the unshed tears in his eyes.

***

If it had been up to Sarah, she never would have chosen a cemetery as Josh's final resting place. In hindsight, it *had* been up to her as Josh's wife, but his parents had felt strongly about putting him to rest in the Mountain Meadows cemetery, the same as his grandparents before him had been. Not that they ever visited since they moved to the city a few years earlier, but they'd cared so much that Sarah had let it happen.

She and Josh had never actually discussed what they wanted when the accident happened—why would they have? They were young and healthy and had their whole lives ahead of them.

Or so they'd thought.

With the arrogance of youth, they'd assumed they were untouchable.

Even though Sarah had never loved the cemetery, and would have preferred to have scattered Josh's ashes into the river the way he would have loved, she'd grown to like it in a way. There was a special kind of peaceful quality. And as silly as it sounded, she did feel a little bit closer to Josh when she sat next to his headstone, with the pine trees at her back, gazing out at the mountains that surrounded them. Not that she'd visited lately. The last time was in January, on his birthday, and she'd brought Rory, who'd built a little snowman next to his headstone.

She put a simple bouquet of daisies that she'd picked from her dad's garden next to his headstone as she sat down and crossed her legs.

Sarah put her hand on the granite, and let the heat of the stone warm her through. "Hey," she said softly. "Happy anniversary." She smiled, but there were no tears. "I bet you thought I forgot."

She chuckled, because it had always been Josh who'd almost forgotten their anniversary. Funny how time changed things.

"It would have been seven years today. Wow, huh?"

Sarah waited a beat, took a breath, and started talking. It had been a long time since she'd sat there and talked to him as if he were sitting next to her. For the first year or two after he'd died, she'd visited regularly. It helped her find some sort of normalcy in the chaos after he'd died. Josh had been her best friend for so long, the hardest part of losing him was knowing she'd never be able to talk to him the way she used to. He'd never again laugh at her for overthinking every little detail about a situation, or talk her down when she got overwhelmed with her to-do list, or even just sit there and nod as he was interested in every little thing while she talked about all the littlest details in her life. He'd been her sounding board. The one person who'd understood her better than anyone else. Josh had always known what she was going to say before she said it.

"It's been a hot summer." She usually started with the weather. "Hotter than that one when we graduated and the air conditioning in the high school went out. Remember that? We had all our classes by the river in the shade because the teachers couldn't focus because of the heat." She smiled at the memory of the way they'd all gather together in the shade of the pines. Hope and Levi would be cuddled up, sneaking kisses and trying not to get caught. She'd always been envious of their easy affection. Josh didn't like to be affectionate in public, and so they'd sat next to each other, not touching and rolling their eyes at their friends.

Sarah shook off the memory. "Well," she continued. "It's hotter than that." She swallowed hard. "In fact, it's so hot I took Rory to the lake." She waited a moment, as if he would reply. It was silly and she continued on. "She loved it, Josh. We built sandcastles and played volleyball and everyone came. It was a proper day at the beach. You would have loved it, too."

She paused and took a deep breath.

"But that's not why I'm here." She drew her knees up to her chest and wrapped her arms around them, hugging herself. "I came because I need to tell you how angry I am with you." She exhaled hard. "You left me and that wasn't fair. I don't know if you meant for it to happen." She squeezed her eyes tight. "I guess I'll never know. But you know as well as I do that running away and going for a swim was bullshit, Josh. It wasn't fair. And I'm so mad and it's time I finally told you so." Sarah worked hard to keep her voice even. "You were my best friend, and I didn't deserve it to end the way it did. Especially because you knew I was right. I know that's true, Josh. You just didn't want to hear it. And it's not fair what you've put me through. The guilt. The shame. The...dammit, I miss you, Josh." Tears slipped down her cheeks then.

"You know how much I loved you. Rory didn't deserve this. You missed so much. And it was all such a waste, because we both deserved so much better. You could have found a woman who lit you up and filled all the empty spaces inside you. And I know you would have." She smiled at the thought because she'd had it before. More than once, she'd pictured the type of wife Josh *should* have had. The wife she couldn't have been for him. "And I deserved to have all that, too."

Sarah dropped her head to her knees and let the tears flow. "It should have been so different. And it's your fault. You left us and it didn't have to be that way. It never should have been that way. I've been so angry at you for so long that I don't even think I realized how mad I was."

She sat that way for a few minutes, letting the tears soak her pants through to her skin. After a while, her tears stopped and Sarah sat up. She wiped her eyes and traced her hand over the carving in the headstone.

Son, Husband, Father

She let her fingers linger on the word in the center.

"I'm angry," she said again. "But you know what? I think I need to be done being angry at you now, Josh. I can't be mad anymore. It's too much. And it won't change anything." She pressed her hand against the stone. "I've felt guilty for too long. It wasn't just you who died that day and maybe that's been the biggest tragedy of all." She swallowed hard, as the feelings she'd kept bottled up for so long took their release. "It's time to move on," she said softly as she let her hand fall away from the stone. "I've been on hold for too long and now I know I'm ready."

She slowly pushed to her feet and stood in front of her dead husband's grave.

"I don't know why you did it, Josh. I'll never know. And I don't think it matters anymore, because I'm letting you go now. I love you. I always will. And I forgive you." She blew a kiss into her hand, bent, and pressed it to the top of the headstone before turning and walking back to her car.

It didn't matter if it was one-sided. It was the hardest conversation she'd ever had. Even harder than the day Josh died. But unlike that day when a weight had settled heavily upon her, it was released now. Sarah had never felt lighter. Things were far from perfect, and she still had no idea what would happen next. But what she did know was that whatever it was that did happen, she would at least have a fighting chance to open her heart.

Chapter Thirteen

SARAH STARED at her reflection in the mirror and blinked hard. She never should have agreed to this.

It was a bad idea.

A very bad idea.

She reached up behind her and fluffed the veil that hung down her back.

A *veil.*

If she would have had any idea that agreeing to do Nicole a favor would have resulted in her spending her Friday night dressed up like a blushing bride, especially after the shit week she'd had, she would have run the other way.

"You look stunning, Sarah!" Faith walked into the bathroom and clasped her hands in excitement. "Thank you so much for doing this. I know that it's probably a little strange."

That didn't even begin to cover it.

But Sarah didn't bother saying anything. Instead, she turned again to the full-length mirror in the bathrooms of the Ever After Ranch barn where she'd been getting ready. "I'm happy to help," she lied. "And I have to admit it is a pretty dress."

It really was, and it fit her perfectly. With a corset back and sweetheart neckline that squeezed her in and pushed her up in all the right places, she did look good despite the extra pounds she couldn't seem to get rid of. "But I don't know why you'd want a single mother, chubby bride in your advertisements."

"Are you kidding me, Sarah?" Faith spun her around. "You are stunning. Curvy in all the right places. You are a gorgeous, real woman, and I'm so excited that it worked out for you to be my bride for this shoot." Faith adjusted Sarah's skirts a little and stood back to admire her. "I'll admit, I never even thought of featuring a same-sex couple in my advertisements, but when Nicole and Amy came to me with the idea, I absolutely loved it. They're beautiful women, who are even more radiant because of the way they look at each other. And you should see how their pictures turned out. We did their shoot earlier this afternoon because Amy had to get back to the restaurant. But they were absolutely perfect. You can really see it when a couple has a connection, and they really have it. Don't you agree?"

Sarah nodded. She had to completely agree. They clearly had each found something special in the other, and even more importantly, it was nice to see love being celebrated in any and all forms. It made Sarah's bruised and battered heart happy to see so much love with her friends. "I think it's wonderful," Sarah admitted to Faith. "And if it means that I have to subject myself to the camera in order to make it happen, then it's all worth it."

Faith clapped her hands and grinned mischievously. "I'm so happy you said that. Because you and your groom will be absolutely perfect. Now, I need you out here for makeup and then onto the shoot, okay?"

She spun on her foot and was halfway out the door when Sarah realized what she'd said.

"Wait," she called after her friend, but either Faith didn't hear her or she'd ignored her because she was gone, and Sarah was left speaking to the empty room. "My groom?"

"Okay, now if you could lean against that tree there." The photographer barked out the direction to Brody, who did his best to follow along. "Just gaze out over the river like you're deep in thought about the biggest day of your life."

Brody was having a hard time staying focused on what the photographer was saying despite the fact that the man was starting to get frustrated with him. The truth was, Brody had been having trouble staying focused on anything for the last few days, and it was a problem that was only growing worse. He'd tried repeatedly to get in touch with Sarah, but she was straight up ignoring him and it was starting to worry him. She hadn't even brought Rory to her soccer practice the night before, letting her dad do it instead. Ed had dodged questions about Sarah, saying she'd had a hard week and was exhausted from work, but Brody knew there was more to it than that.

It was him.

She was avoiding him because—

"Brody!" Faith was yelling at him.

He shook his head to clear it and focus on his friend, who was marching toward him.

"I need you to focus. Dan's telling me that you're not taking direction and you look sad."

"I'm not sad."

"But you're not taking direction."

He shrugged. "Probably not."

She tipped her head and glared at him. "Could you try, please? I need my groom to be on point when his bride gets here. And she's almost ready."

His bride. Brody almost laughed at the idea. Especially

considering it was supposed to be Amy. "And who *is* my bride, anyway? Amy said she was going to find someone."

Faith grinned. "She didn't tell you?"

"Obviously not."

"Oh, perfect." She giggled a little and scribbled something onto her clipboard. "Then you'll be surprised when she walks down the aisle. It'll look so real."

Brody tried not to get annoyed with her. After all, Faith was just doing her job and trying to get a marketing campaign off the ground to help her business. He could respect that. He didn't need to be so pouty about it all. Besides, if he just focused, it would be over sooner and he could go figure out a way to get through to Sarah.

"In fact," Faith looked at her cell phone, "Logan just texted. Turns out the bride is ready." She grabbed Brody's hand and walked toward the ceremony space that had been set up, complete with an arch he assumed he was supposed to stand under.

No guests, though. At least he wouldn't have to worry about faking his excitement to marry his pretend bride in front of any other people.

"Okay," Faith said. "You stand here. Look expectant, okay? You need to look nervous and excited and all the things a groom would feel. As soon as you see her, pretend she is the love of your life and smile like she is the most beautiful woman in the world and you can't wait to make her your wife."

He nodded. There was no point doing anything else.

"Great. Okay. Here she comes."

Behind her, Brody noticed the golf cart that Faith usually used to get around the property pull up with Logan behind the wheel, and a bride next to him.

"So maybe stand with your hands clasped and your head bowed. Look up when I tell you to, okay? That way maybe your reaction will be a little more natural."

"Whatever," Brody mumbled. He did as he was instructed and tried to channel some positive thoughts. *What would it feel like to see Sarah walking down the aisle toward him?*

Damn.

No. He couldn't let his mind go there. There'd be no coming back from it. But still, he couldn't shake the image from his head. *Sarah in a white dress. Sarah with a bouquet of flowers in her hand, clutched tightly to keep her from trembling. Sarah with a smile lighting up her face because she looked down the aisle, at him.*

It was a nice thought, but so far from reality that he actually chuckled.

Somewhere, he heard Faith tell him to look up, which he did.

Brody blinked. The smile on his face first grew wider, and then fell away as he realized that the woman walking down the aisle toward him *was* the bride of his dreams.

Only she wasn't smiling.

"Smile!" Faith yelled out, on cue. "You're getting married. You're happy. This is the best day of your lives!"

Sarah did not look happy. Still, she smiled. At least, she tried. But by the time she got down the aisle to where he stood, more than ready for her, her lips were pressed into a hard line.

"You look gorgeous."

"I didn't know you were going to be…" She shook her head.

"You look gorgeous," he said again.

Faith was hollering out directions, and as much as Brody would have liked to pick Sarah up and carry her out into the woods where they could finally talk through everything, he'd promised Faith he'd do the pictures. So, Brody reached for her hand. "I'm glad you're here."

She hesitated, and looked at his outstretched hand.

For a moment, Brody was sure she was going to pick up her skirts and run down the aisle away from him. Finally, after what felt like an eternity, she put her hand in his. He squeezed it a little and smiled at her, but there was nothing but hardness in her eyes.

"I wish I could say the same."

Sarah willed herself to calm down. Through clenched teeth, she did her best to slow her breathing.

She was going to kill Faith. How could she surprise her like this? With *Brody?*

She couldn't do it. She couldn't stand next to him, wearing a wedding gown, and pretend that everything was okay when it was so very far from it.

Sarah looked to where her friend stood with Logan and the photographer, smiling blissfully, as if she had no idea the inner turmoil Sarah was in.

Which, to be fair, she probably didn't. After all, how could she? Sarah hadn't spoken with anyone about what was going on with her and Brody.

Except maybe Josh. But that didn't count. And even so, she hadn't actually *told* Josh that she was falling in love with another man.

Love.

Dammit. She exhaled hard. She was so screwed.

Despite her conversation with her deceased husband earlier in the week, and the weight that had been lifted because of it, she still hadn't been able to bring herself to answer any of Brody's voicemails or text messages.

What would she say?

That she was sorry?

That their night together had been both the best and most terrifying of her life?

That she was falling for him?

That she was still so angry at him for being careless with Rory?

That she missed him?

That she was confused?

All of the above.

She needed to get out of there. There was no way she could stand there and pretend that not only was everything okay with Brody but that they were a happy couple on their wedding day. Sarah looked around, frantic for an escape route, and when he took her hand in his, for a second she was sure her knees would give out. It was too much.

But she'd promised Faith. If she ran out now, she'd look completely crazy. It would only make everything worse.

"I'm glad you're here," Brody said when he reached out for her hand.

She knew she was being hard. She knew she was being a bitch, but it was just self-preservation. "I wish I could say the same."

Sarah forced herself to look at her *groom*, careful to keep her expression neutral.

Damn.

He looked amazing. Of course, Brody always looked amazing. But in a tuxedo, he was on a whole different level. When he took her hand in his, she felt herself melt a little.

"Look into each other's eyes."

Sarah took a deep breath.

Brody moved closer to her and cupped her cheek with his hand. She knew they were only supposed to be acting, but his touch on her skin warmed her in a way that made her feel complete. Reflexively, she leaned into it.

"I've missed you, Sarah," Brody whispered as he leaned in closer.

She closed her eyes to keep from looking at him, afraid her resolve would break.

Vaguely, Sarah was aware of Faith yelling directions, but she was completely focused on maintaining her composure, which was becoming increasingly difficult.

"I hope you know how sorry I am, Sarah."

She opened her eyes. "Sorry?"

If he said one word about being sorry for the night they spent together...mostly because it was both the best night of her life and the worst... And she hadn't been able to stop thinking about it.

"For..." He hesitated. "Well, for everything, Sarah. I don't know what happened the other night, but I—"

She stiffened. "You don't know what—"

"Okay, kiss!"

Kiss?

Instinctively, Sarah pulled back as Faith called out the instruction. *There was no way she was going to—*

Brody pulled her back and then his lips were on hers in a very chaste and very pretend kiss.

When he stepped back, she glared at him.

Brody shrugged. "It's for the photos," he said by way of explanation.

"*That* was your kiss?"

Both Brody and Sarah looked to where Logan, who stood next to Faith and the photographer, was laughing, as if he'd just seen the funniest thing ever. Which maybe he had. Because Sarah didn't need to see the photo to know that it was probably the worst *just married* kiss in history. Pretend or otherwise.

She looked to Brody, and for a second, contemplated a do-over because she was sure they could do better. Hell, she *knew* they could do better. But before she could even let herself fully entertain the thought, Brody laughed.

He laughed.

She took a step to the side, away from him as Faith and Logan approached them.

"Okay," Faith started. "I know this might be a little

awkward, because it's a photo shoot and all." She looked between them and smiled. "But it *is* supposed to look like a real wedding. Complete with all the feels and emotions and…well, all of it. Do you get what I'm saying?"

Brody nodded, but Sarah shook her head. "I don't—"

"What she's trying to say is that the kiss needs to have passion," Logan interrupted. "Feeling and conviction. You need to look like you're actually really in to the other person. Like their very existence is what keeps you going." Sarah fought the urge to roll her eyes, but Logan was just getting started. "You need to sell people on the idea of love and passion. Your kiss needs to have heat. It needs to…here. Let me show you."

Before anyone could react, least of all Faith, Logan had wrapped his arms around her, pulled her close, and was kissing her with enough heat to make all of them blush.

Chapter Fourteen

SHE SHOULD PUSH HIM OFF.

She should slap him across the face.

She should do a lot of things, but all Faith wanted to do was kiss him back. And that's exactly what she did.

For the moment, it didn't matter that they were in the middle of a professional photo shoot, or that Brody and Sarah stood a few feet away from them, no doubt as shocked as she was. Okay, maybe not as much as she was.

Nothing mattered except for the feel of Logan's lips on hers, his hands on her, and every single sensation that he'd ignited within her body. Vaguely, she heard a moan, and realized that it had come from her. But still, she didn't care.

She leaned into the kiss. Her own hands came to wrap around him.

There were so many reasons she shouldn't be letting the kiss happen.. But still, Faith couldn't make herself pull away from Logan. Instead, she deepened the kiss and pressed herself closer.

And then, just as abruptly as it had started, it was over.

"And that," she heard Logan say, "is how it's done."

Her fingers fluttered to her lips as Faith came to the realization of what had just happened. It wasn't the first time they'd shared a kiss. The last time being in the middle of an event they were hosting. Also, not professional. But this...this was next level. And entirely inappropriate. She glared at Logan and worked hard not to slap him across the face. There'd been enough lack of professionalism for one day.

Instead of saying all the things she really wanted to say, Faith looked to Sarah and Brody. Something was going on between the two of them, that much was certain. Despite the fact that Sarah insisted they were only friends, it didn't take a genius to see the way they looked at each other.

Usually.

Today was different.

Of course, they'd had that big blow-up at the beach the weekend before... With a sigh, Faith jumped in. "Okay, enough. What's going on between the two of you?"

They each looked to the other and shrugged.

"Look," Faith continued. "I get that you're upset with him for what happened on Sunday." Sarah turned a bright shade of pink while she was talking, but didn't say anything to argue the point. "But you need to get over it. At least for the next hour or so, please. Can you just pretend to be desperately, hopelessly in love?"

Brody nodded and the faintest trace of a smile crossed his face. "Oh, I think I can handle that, no problem." He looked to Sarah, but she was determinedly looking straight ahead, so Faith focused on her.

"Sarah?" she prompted. "Can *you* do that? For me? For a hour? Pretend that Brody is the love of your life and you can't live without him. And then you can go back to being..." She fluttered her hand around. "Whatever it is that you're doing."

She waited a beat and finally her friend nodded. "Of course," Sarah muttered. "I'm sorry. I'll try harder."

"Thank you." She looked to Dan Drummond, the photographer she'd hired, who was looking vaguely amused, and Faith couldn't be sure whether it was the scene that was currently playing out before him, or the one from a moment before that he found so amusing. Not that it mattered. She'd gotten a great deal on the shoot because she'd agreed to let him use a few pictures and do a feature on weddings for an online article on *Weddings Weekly*. She'd hadn't been totally worried about the details. He was a good photographer and it was a good price. So, if Dan was entertained by whatever was going on here, she didn't care. She had a job to do. "Let's do this." She waved her clipboard in the air. "It shouldn't be that hard."

After another hour or so, they had managed to finally get enough shots that Faith was fairly sure they had what they needed. It had been a struggle at times, but Faith was sure they got enough shots to make it all work. She thanked Dan, who promised to send her the final shots by the end of the following week and excused Sarah, who seemed relieved to be finished and away from Brody. Who seemed reluctant to let Sarah walk away. There was definitely something going on there, but for the life of her, Faith couldn't figure out what it was. One minute they seemed like they were finally going to figure out what everyone else knew and make it official, and the next, it was as if they couldn't stand the sight of each other.

She waited until everyone was gone, and then—more than ready to pour herself a glass of wine and kick her feet up on the porch—she grabbed her clipboard and was walking through the barn when Logan appeared in front of her.

"That went pretty well, don't you think?"

She jumped back and wielded her clipboard.

"Don't hit me." Logan laughed.

Despite herself, Faith found herself smiling. A detail that left her conflicted. Logan had done nothing but infuriate her since she was sixteen years old. *And turn her on.* She forced that particular line of thought from her mind. It didn't matter if his kiss earlier had left her toes curled and her panties a little damp. He was *Logan.*

"I should do a lot more than hit you for what you pulled earlier." She hugged her clipboard tight and pushed past him to the door.

He grabbed her arm before she could reach it, and spun her around, backing her up against the wall. "Like…you should maybe kiss me again?"

He stood so close, Faith could smell the sharp, clean scent of his soap mixed with the earthy muck that was distinctly Logan. Despite herself, her breath came in short puffs as her heart rate raced.

He leaned in closer.

It would be so easy to kiss him. To give in to the feelings that, despite her best efforts to stop them, continued to grow for this man who made her so crazy.

How bad could it be?

Very bad.

It could be very bad. And it would be very bad if she gave in to those feelings. For so many reasons.

One…they worked together.

Two…

Damn. Why couldn't she think of a two?

She pulled in a sharp breath and Logan's lips twitched up in a cocky grin as he leaned in.

Shit.

Two…he was *Logan Langdon.*

Right before his lips connected with hers, she ducked to the side.

There was no way she could let herself go there. Not with

Logan.

She snuck out the barn door into the fresh air, leaving him hanging.

No.

Not when he had the ability to make her feel so many things with just one kiss.

No way.

"Faith!"

She was being childish, she knew it, but still Faith didn't turn around. Maybe she could pretend that she didn't hear him calling after her. Or that she'd basically just run away from him.

"I know you can hear me."

She stopped and turned around.

"And now you see me," Logan added with a chuckle. But the laughter faded a moment later when he added, "What the hell is going on? Why are you being so difficult about all of this?"

"About what?"

"You know exactly what."

She tilted her head in question.

"You need me to say it?" He crossed his arms over his chest.

Faith had to work hard to ignore the sensations that flashed through her at the sight of his thick bicep muscles. *To have those arms wrapped around her and—*

"Us," he said, interrupting her train of thought. "Why are you being so fucking difficult about *us.*"

"There is no us, Logan." Faith hoped her words sounded more convincing as she spoke them than they did in her head. "We work together. That's it."

"No." He wasn't giving up. "You know that's not it. That's *never* been it and you're just—"

"Faith?"

They both turned to see Sarah walking toward them. She had a giant garment bag cradled in her arms. "Can I talk to you for a second?" she asked as she got closer.

"No."

"Of course."

They spoke at the same time, and Faith glared at Logan and turned back to Sarah, who had stopped walking and looked cautiously between them. "Of course you can talk to me. Logan and I were just finishing up here." She took the dress from Sarah's arms and handed it to Logan. "Would you make yourself helpful and hang this up in the back room for me?" She smiled as sweetly as she could manage despite the fact that her heart was racing just looking at the man.

What was it about him that made her so crazy? And scared the hell out of her?

Logan hesitated, looking first to Sarah and then back at Faith, before taking the garment bag from her. "Of course, *boss*. Happy to help. And we'll finish our conversation later."

Faith waited until Logan had disappeared back inside the barn before grabbing Sarah's arm and hurriedly leading her toward the house on the other side of the parking space. "I'm desperate for a glass of wine. Come on."

A few minutes later, they were settled on Faith's porch with a glass of pinot noir. "Sorry about that," Faith said. "And I didn't even ask you if you had a few minutes. I just kind of hijacked you for a drink."

Sarah laughed. "I don't mind, honestly. I think I could use one. Or two." She shook her head and looked back to Faith. "But I didn't mean to interrupt, Faith. It looked like you two were in the middle of something."

"No more than usual." Faith took a long sip of the liquid and let it slide down her throat to warm her insides. She didn't want to talk about Logan. Not with anyone. Not when she couldn't figure things out on her own. "What was it you needed to talk about? Is everything okay?"

"Honestly?"

"Of course."

Sarah took a deep breath and exhaled slowly. "Yes," she finally answered.

It was bullshit and they both knew it. But just like Faith didn't want to talk, she wasn't going to push her friend.

"But I did want to apologize for being a little difficult in the photo shoot today," Sarah added. "I wasn't expecting my partner to be Brody, and I had a hard time with...well, it was all just a little unexpected. And I'm sorry if it caused you any troubles at all with your pictures. I know you're working hard to get the ad campaign off the ground and you didn't need to deal with—"

"What *is* going on with you and Brody, Sarah?" Maybe the question was too up front, and maybe she should have been more sensitive about it, but Faith didn't care. Something was clearly bothering her friend, so she might as well get to the bottom of it. Besides, it was so much easier than dealing with her own issues.

"Nothing," Sarah answered after a moment. She took a noticeably large gulp of her wine and looked out over the porch. "I think I've shut off the possibility of that forever."

From what Faith had seen, there was pretty much zero chance of that. Not with the way Brody looked at her. That was a man in love, there was no doubt. Hell, if even a woman like Faith, who had spent the majority of her life cynical about the entire idea of it, could see it in the way Brody looked at Sarah—and if she were honest, the way she looked back at him—then it was definitely there. "That's highly doubtful." Faith lifted her glass of wine and grinned at her friend. "Not from what I've seen."

"You haven't seen it all."

"Obviously not. But I don't think I need to."

Sarah raised her glass to her lips but lowered it before taking another sip. "Can I tell you something?" She didn't look at Faith, but straight out to the trees at the edge of the property. She didn't wait for an answer before continuing. "I'm in love with him."

Faith's face transformed as a smile took over her face. She *knew* it.

"In fact," Sarah continued, "I have never felt like this about anyone before. No one." She shook her head and looked at Faith. "Not even Josh."

The comment should have surprised her, but somehow it didn't. "That's okay, Sarah. Really, it is."

"I know." She looked sad, and not at all like a woman who'd just realized she was in love.

Faith waited for a few minutes but Sarah didn't look as though she was going to add to her comment. "Forgive me," she said cautiously. "But if you love him more than anyone else…and he clearly loves you, then…well, I guess I'm not sure what the problem is."

She watched as her friend inhaled a deep breath and blew it out slowly. "You're going to think I'm crazy."

"Absolutely not."

Sarah managed a small smile. "I've spent a lot of time being mad," she said after a moment. "At Josh, for the way things ended."

Faith thought it an odd choice of words, but she didn't interrupt. It was clear that Sarah needed to talk.

"And at myself for…well…for so much. I've been really scared, and just when I let myself think that Brody could be the one…well, he scared me, Faith. That moment at the lake, it just seemed too real that I could love and then lose again. And I got so scared. I just don't know if I can do it a second time."

Faith absorbed what she was saying and finally she reached

across the table and took Sarah's hand. "Do you want to know what I think?" She didn't wait for an answer before continuing. "I think that it's okay to be scared. But you already know that. And yes, something terrible could happen again. I mean, no one knows the future. But from where I'm sitting, the most terrible thing that could happen is not ever taking that chance."

Sarah looked up into her eyes and Faith could see the spark of recognition there.

"But you already know that, too." Faith smiled. "Maybe hanging on to some sort of misguided anger with Brody is your way of thinking that you're protecting your heart. But from what I can see, your heart will be pretty safe with him."

Faith didn't even recognize herself or the words coming out of her mouth, but as crazy as it seemed, she believed every word. And she could see it was resonating with Sarah, too.

Even so, Sarah pulled her hand away and lifted her glass to her lips. "It's not that I don't think you have a point." She stared at the glass for a moment. "I just…well, I guess I just don't know."

"You will." Faith smiled because she believed it to be true. Still, as they sat and finished their wine, Faith started to question all of her changing beliefs. Sure, being back in town and at Ever After had definitely given her different ideas about love, but maybe she'd been too hasty.

Because if Sarah was any kind of indication of what it felt like to be in love and have feelings she'd never had before, she should definitely rethink the whole thing.

Chapter Fifteen

"GO, RORY, GO! RUN!" Sarah never would have thought she'd end up being one of those parents who screamed from the stands at their child on the field. But here she was. And she was loving every single minute of it. Besides, if a final championship game wasn't a reason to get up and scream and cheer, she didn't know what was.

Rory kicked the ball and just missed the net. The referee blew the whistle and everyone regrouped.

Sarah sat down and looked to Byron, who was sitting next to her. "This is great, isn't it?"

"Better than any professional game I've ever been to." He laughed. "Not that I've been to a lot of professional soccer games."

Sarah laughed. She was having more fun at the soccer game in Cedar Springs than she'd had in weeks. The kids were playing well and, more importantly, they were laughing and cheering and having a great time.

Even the fact that she'd handed off the wind-up party to Audrey wasn't getting Sarah down. In fact, she'd found that with everything else going on in her life, not having to pretend to give a crap about impressing a woman who would never be impressed by her had lifted a weight off her shoulders. Besides, at the end of the day, a wind-up party was a wind-up party. The kids were going to have a great time, and that was all that mattered. Sarah had picked up two dozen cupcakes from Sweetie Pies that morning, each with individual soccer balls on them, for the picnic party they were having after the game. The kids would love them.

"Such a beautiful day, too," Byron was saying.

She'd been worried that after their *date*, things might be awkward between them, but she needn't have worried. They were still good friends. Maybe more so now that they'd tried and failed at any attempt of dating.

"Having the picnic up at the lake was a great idea. Thanks for organizing."

"I didn't organize," she corrected him, taking a moment to process what he'd just said. "I got a little overwhelmed with… work. I let Audrey take over." She shook her head a little. "What did you say about the lake? The wind-up party is at the lake?"

Despite the heat of the day, her entire body had grown cold instantly and she couldn't feel her toes. She'd only heard that the party would be a picnic. Come to think of it, the location hadn't really been discussed. She'd assumed it would be right there on the field after the game. But she'd never asked, and Audrey definitely hadn't offered the information.

But why?

She knew exactly why Audrey had done it. Or, in this case, hadn't done it. Because she knew how Sarah would react. It didn't even matter if she'd done it maliciously. Which, for her own sanity, Sarah couldn't let herself believe. They may have a little feud, but not even Audrey would stoop to that. She had to believe it.

But malicious or not, there was no way Sarah was going to the lake. Not after what happened the week before.

No. Way.

Sarah's face grew hot, but she refused to let her emotions show. Not there. Not in the middle of the game.

Instead, she refocused on the action on the field as the Glacier Falls Grizzlies stole the ball from one of the Cedar Springs Cougars and started to run down the field. "Go, Grizzlies!"

But the other parents were screaming, too. And not in encouragement.

"The other way!" Byron yelled next to her. "Go the other way." He looked at her with such a look of despair that Sarah couldn't help but burst out laughing. Byron's eyes opened wide and then he, too, burst out laughing, while his daughter ran straight for the wrong goal.

From the sidelines, Brody turned around and when he saw them laughing, he shook his head in a "what can you do" gesture and grinned broadly. It was such a small thing, but it took her off guard and she looked away, the laughter dying on her lips.

She'd been worried about seeing Brody at the soccer game. She'd been so terrible at the photo shoot on Friday night and although she knew she should apologize, she couldn't bring herself to do it. After all, it wasn't her fault that she'd been taken off guard and pretty much hijacked into the whole situation. How did he expect her to react?

Fortunately, Annie figured out she was running in the wrong direction, turned and headed down the field toward the proper goal. She didn't score, but the Grizzlies went on to play a strong game and ultimately won over the Cougars by one goal. The crowd erupted in screams and cheering as the parents ran onto the field to hug their daughters.

"That was an awesome game, kiddo!"

"We won! I can't believe we won!"

"Believe it, Rory," Ed, who'd been watching from the side-lines, said as he wrapped his granddaughter in a hug. "You girls worked hard and you did it. You should be proud."

"We get cupcakes!"

Both Sarah and Ed laughed. At six years old, that was all that was really important. Maybe the kids had it right.

"You sure do. Now go cheer with your team." Sarah didn't bother pointing out that win or lose, there would have been cupcakes. It didn't matter. Instead, as Rory ran off to join her team, Sarah turned to her father. "Can you take Rory to the wind-up party?"

Ed gave her a curious look.

"There's something I need to do," she said as a way of explanation. Uncomfortable with the lie, she added, "It's at the lake."

"Ah." Ed nodded in understanding. But then he quickly shook his head. "But I can't."

"You can't?" She did her best not to look stressed, but she was pretty sure she'd failed at the effort. "Why not? What are you doing?"

Ed laughed. "I have plans, Sarah. And, no. Before you ask. I cannot cancel them." His expression softened. "Besides, you should go. It'll be fun and—"

"It's at the *lake*, Dad." She hadn't told her dad about the last time she'd been at the lake, but no doubt her daughter had filled him in on all the embarrassing details. "I don't know if I—"

"You can," he said firmly. "And you will." He looked over her shoulder toward the field. "You're stronger than you think. It's all okay."

Sarah turned to see where he was looking, but could only see the group of kids and...Brody. She whipped her head around to look at her dad again, but he was only smiling.

"Trust yourself, Sarah. It's time."

When Brody had offered months ago to volunteer as coach for the Glacier Falls Grizzlies, he'd never expected to fall in love the way he had. But as he stood on the wooden table in the picnic area of Cedar Springs Lake where the wind-up party had been set up, and looked around at all the little faces of his championship athletes, he realized with a smile that falling in love was exactly what had happened.

"I can't tell you how proud I am of every single one of you," he said. "You've all worked so hard. Coming to every practice and putting in your best effort every single time. You've all come so far and really improved your soccer skills. But most importantly, you've had so much fun doing it, and it shows. A team that has fun together and plays like a unit is what's most important. And you all have demonstrated that so perfectly. The friendships you've made here will last a lifetime, and I hope to see you all back next season. Thank you so much for letting me be your coach."

A cheer went up among the athletes and their parents, followed by someone yelling out, "Three cheers for Coach Brody."

"Hip hip hooray!"

"Hip hip hooray!"

"Hip hip hooray!"

"Okay, that's enough of that." Brody blushed and waved away the accolades. "Let's eat and have some fun!"

Next to him on the ground, Audrey whispered something, so he bent to receive the message before announcing to the crowd, "Kids, the wind is starting to pick up, and it looks like a storm might be coming in, so make sure you stay in the picnic area here, and on the playground equipment right over there. The beach and the lake are off-limits unless you're with your parent." He scanned the crowd and found Sarah standing toward the back. He looked her straight in the eye and offered her a little smile, but she looked away. "Okay," he said once more. "Let's party!"

The moment he hopped down from the table, he moved through the crowd, doing his best to smile and accept the compliments and well wishes from parents without appearing rude as he tried to go as fast as possible to where Sarah had been standing.

"Hey." She had her back to him, but Brody could tell she wasn't surprised to hear his voice. "I'm glad I caught you."

Slowly, she turned around. She wasn't smiling, but she didn't look outwardly hostile toward him either, so he'd take that as a win. "Good game, Coach."

"Thanks. But I can't take any credit. The girls are awesome." He nodded to where Rory and a few of her friends, including Audrey's daughter, Clara, were stuffing cupcakes into their mouths. "They seem to be enjoying their rewards."

Sarah smiled then.

"Great party," he added when she didn't say anything else. "You did a great job. I'm sorry I didn't help out the way I said I would. But with everything going on…well…anyway. It looks great. But I'm not going to lie. I'm a little surprised you decided to have it here."

"I can't take any credit for the party or the location." She crossed her arms over her chest. "There was just too much going on," she continued. "So I let Audrey take over the planning." She didn't have to say what was *going on*, because Brody knew he was responsible at least in part to adding to her stress level in some way. "I had no idea it would be at the lake."

At least that made sense.

"How are you with—"

"I don't think this is the time…" She turned away.

But it was the time. It had to be the time, because there was never going to be a better time, and if he didn't talk to her about what the hell was going on between them and soon, he was going to explode.

"You know what?" His tone must have caught her attention because she turned around again and tilted her head. "This is exactly the time, Sarah. We need to talk and I'm not going to take no for an answer. Not anymore."

Her lips pressed together and Brody was sure she was going to refuse him again. Instead, she closed her eyes and let out a long breath before looking up. "Okay."

"Okay?"

She nodded and glanced toward Rory, who was still sitting with the other girls and happily snacking away. "Okay," she said again. "You're right, we should talk." She looked back at him. "But not here."

Before he could say anything, Sarah started to walk through the trees, away from the picnic area. He followed obediently and as soon as they were a safe distance away from prying eyes, she turned and looked him straight in the eyes. "Brody, I don't know—"

"Let me talk. Please."

She was so beautiful, standing there in her shorts and T-shirt; she was even more gorgeous than a few days earlier when she'd been wearing a stunning wedding gown. The woman was so intensely beautiful, it literally took his breath away. But it was so much more than the way she looked. It was how she made him feel inside. The last few weeks had been an intense roller coaster ride of the highest highs when he'd made love to her, and the lowest of lows when she looked him straight in the eyes and told him to leave. It was time to get off the fucking ride.

Brody reached for her hand, and she didn't pull away. He cradled it between his and held tight. "Sarah, I can't do this anymore. I can't pretend that everything is normal with us, when it is anything but."

"I know, I'm—"

"Please. Let me finish." She closed her mouth and he continued. "I know you're scared, Sarah." She squeezed her eyes shut for a moment, but opened them again. "And I'm not really sure what it is that has you so spooked, but I need to tell you exactly how I feel. And if you still want to push me away and turn your back on what's happening between us and everything that could be, then I'll walk away. I'll leave you alone if that's what you want. But either way, I'm going to need an answer because I can't keep doing this. I can't keep feeling the way I'm feeling and not know what's going on with you. I need to call my shot." He paused and took a breath. "Will you hear what I have to say?"

She nodded and Brody didn't waste any more time.

"Sarah Lewis, I love you."

She sucked in a sharp gasp of air and wrapped her arms around her waist, but he didn't stop.

"But more than that, I am *in* love with you." He took a step closer to her and prayed she wouldn't pull away. Brody had been bold when he said he'd walk away if she didn't feel the same, but he'd meant it. He would. Because he had to. There was no way he'd be able to continue their relationship in the same way they had been going if she didn't feel the same. As painful as it would be to walk away from her, to be so close yet so far away would be far more painful. "Sarah, I've been in love with you for a very long time. And I think you're in love with me, too."

It wasn't even a question.

Of course she was in love with Brody. It had taken her a

little bit to see it, of course, but once she had…well, that was the whole problem. She was desperately in love with him. So much so, she'd been in physical pain since she'd kicked him out of her house a week earlier. She ached for his lips on hers. For his hands on her body. For his arms wrapped around her, holding her tight. Hell, just for his physical presence close to hers.

As much as her heart was racing since he'd taken her hands in his, there was also a calmness that had settled over her just being close to him again. It was a strange push and pull between her heart and her brain.

Hundreds of things raced through Sarah's brain. And if she let herself, she'd come up with a dozen reasons about why she shouldn't let Brody in. Hell, she'd already been doing a pretty good job of that. But she didn't need to feel guilty anymore. Not for Josh. Not for Brody. And not for wanting more.

She was allowed to want more. She was allowed to *feel* more.

She knew that now.

But still, something held her back.

Only this time, it wasn't guilt. It was fear.

Sarah knew if she opened her mouth, she'd tell Brody exactly how she felt about him, too. But then everything would change. There'd be stakes. There'd be something to lose again.

Could she risk it?

Losing Josh had been the hardest thing she'd ever done.

But did it kill you?

No.

She'd survived the loss of her husband.

Sarah took a deep breath and let her lungs fill with the fresh scent of ozone on the air as the wind picked up and the storm that had been threatening grew closer.

She could survive anything that life threw at her. She knew that now.

But the only thing she couldn't survive was losing out on the chance at something because she was scared.

There would be no coming back from that.

And she was done being afraid. She was done with putting her life on hold because of a terrible accident. One that wasn't her fault. No matter how she'd beat herself up for it over the years, she knew that now. Hell, she'd known it for a long time, but she'd finally allowed herself to admit it.

Josh's death wasn't her fault. Wanting more wasn't wrong. And Brody *was* more. And he was right here.

Being upset with him wasn't keeping anyone safe. It was keeping them apart.

She exhaled slowly, emptying her lungs and focusing her thoughts.

Brody stood before her. Patient and waiting.

"You know it's not just you, right?"

Sarah blinked at his question, and Brody smiled slowly before explaining.

"It's not just you who I love," he said. "I need you to know how much I care about Rory, too."

Sarah's heart clenched a little.

"I love her like my own daughter, Sarah. And that feeling only grows stronger every day. Last week," he continued, "when you thought I'd taken my eyes off her in the lake…" He dropped his head and shook it a little before looking up into her eyes.

Sarah could feel the pain in his voice as he spoke.

"It killed me that you could, even for a second, think I'd ever put her in harm's way. I love that girl, Sarah. I will do everything in my power to keep her safe. Always. I need you to know that. I need you to understand how much I love *both* of you."

She did know. *Damnit.* Did she ever.

Tears slipped from her eyes before she could stop them and she nodded, unable to form the words that she needed in order to properly express to him exactly what she needed to. Instead, the tears came harder and she couldn't seem to stop them.

"Sarah?" Brody's voice was laced with concern, but she still couldn't seem to stem the flow of emotion. "Is that...you don't..." He nodded. "Okay, I understand." He squeezed her hand one more time and released her. "I'll keep my promise."

What?

"If you don't feel the same, I'll leave you—"

"No." His words shocked her into action. Brody stopped mid-turn and looked at her. It was such a ridiculous misunderstanding, she couldn't help it; to her horror, she started to laugh. "No," she said through a mixture of tears and laughter. "That's not..."

Sarah sighed. She was making such a mess of things.

She took two steps toward him and cupped his face in her hands, feeling the scruff of his unshaved whiskers against her palms. She held him close and kissed him thoroughly. "I'm so in love with you, too."

"Really?"

She sucked her bottom lip between her teeth. "I'm so sorry, Brody. About everything. I've been so confused and scared and on Friday, when I saw you...I don't know. It was all too much. I hadn't processed everything yet and..."

He put a finger to her lips. "It's okay."

But she shook her head. "No. It's not, Brody. I haven't been fair to you. I'm really, really sorry. It was all just so much to work through and to be honest, I never thought I'd be in this situation again. Or...ever."

It still felt strange to think that what she was feeling for Brody was so different than what she had with Josh. Strange. But it no longer felt wrong.

"And I need to be honest," she added after a moment. "I'm still absolutely terrified of losing you. Or Rory or…well…" She smiled, because it was time to let those worries go. "I can't live my life in fear, and the one thing I'm scared of more than anything else is missing out on what we could have."

Brody's face split into the widest smile she'd ever seen. His eyes sparkled as he pulled her close so his lips were barely more than inches away from hers. "Baby, it's not what we *could* have. It's what we *will* have. And what we're going to have together will be magic." He kissed her then, and it *was* magic.

The entire world fell away as they melted into each other. It had taken a lot, maybe more than she'd ever thought it would, but finally she'd gotten to the point where she could open up and be capable of this kind of love. She wasn't going to lose anything or anyone. She *could* have it all and feel it all.

And more than that, she deserved it.

The wind whipped around them, but Sarah was anything but cold as Brody deepened the kiss, and Sarah willingly met his need with her own, completely in the moment with him. Together.

Until a scream that made Sarah's blood instantly run cold shattered their bubble.

Chapter Sixteen

THE SCREAM CAME from the picnic area. Before Brody could even fully comprehend what he'd heard, Sarah had torn herself from his arms and was running through the trees toward the party.

He was right on her heels as they broke through the forest into the clearing of picnic tables, parents, and kids.

Sarah's instincts were in high gear as she scanned the group. "Rory?"

The little girl wasn't where they'd left her, sitting with Clara, eating cupcakes.

Brody took in the scene.

The wind had come up in full force, blowing paper cups and tablecloths all around the space. Some kids were crying and some were cheering as booming thunder shook the earth and flashes of lightning appeared overhead. Parents were yelling and doing their best to gather things before the wind scattered everything, but not all the parents were working to contain the scene. Audrey was shouting and spinning in frantic circles. A small group of parents were trying to calm her down. And Sarah made a beeline directly for her.

She knew. Instinctively, she *knew*.

Brody ran after her.

"They're missing! Missing... I don't know..." Audrey was yelling, hysterical.

Brody's heart stopped for a moment as he realized what she was saying.

"Missing?" Sarah demanded. She grabbed Audrey by the shoulders and forced her to look at her. "What do you mean, missing? Who's missing? Where's Rory? Audrey!"

Audrey, tears streaming down her cheeks, shook her head. "I don't know," she said through sobs. "Rory and Clara— they're gone. They were here one minute. Right over there." She pointed to exactly the spot where Brody and Sarah had left them earlier. "And when the wind picked up, everyone...well... when I looked to find them, they were gone."

Brody didn't need to hear anymore. He looked around one more time, hoping that maybe the girls had been hiding under a picnic table. But of course they weren't.

He turned in the direction of the lake and *knew*. Of course they'd go exactly where they weren't supposed to. Sarah followed his gaze; her hand clamped down on his arm when she came to the same realization he had. Her mouth opened in terror. Brody grabbed her hand and without a word, together they took off running through the trees and toward the beach.

The calm, idyllic lake they'd visited last week was gone. Replaced by frothing, angry white caps. It looked more like the middle of the ocean than a small glacier-fed lake in the mountains.

"Not the lake. Not the lake." Sarah froze. "Oh my God, Brody. The girls!"

He'd seen it at the same time. The girls were huddled on the swimming platform anchored in the lake that was pitching and tossing them around in the wild wind and waves. Their cries could barely be heard over the whistling wind and the crashes of thunder overhead. The rain had started to fall while they'd run to the beach and the big, cold drops came in sheets, blurring their vision and at times making it hard to tell where the lake ended and the sky began.

How did they get out there?

It didn't even matter.

They needed a boat. It was the only safe way to get to the girls. But, of course, all the boats had been safely secured long before the storm. There wasn't even a rowboat to be found and no way was Brody going to waste any time searching for one.

He ran through the rain, toward the shore, stripping off his T-shirt as he went.

"Brody! No!" Sarah was right behind him. "It's too…"

He turned to her and saw the horror on her face. This was her worst nightmare coming to life and he couldn't even begin to imagine what was going through her head. Quickly, he crossed back to her. "It's okay, Sarah." Quickly, he held her face in his hands and kissed her hard. "I'll get her. I'll keep her safe. I promise."

Water streaked down her face but he couldn't be sure whether it was tears or rain. "I'll get her," he promised.

And then he was on the move again. He scanned the shoreline and found a paddleboard that had been abandoned. It would have to do. Brody hauled it into the lake and jumped on, lying flat on his stomach. He paddled with both arms and fought hard against the crashing waves. Beneath him, the board bounced and slammed. He could hardly see as water splashed into his face, blinding him.

It was taking too long. He should have been at the swim platform by now.

Sarah's face, full of horror and fear right before he'd headed into the lake, was seared into his memory. He wouldn't give up. He couldn't. And he'd meant what he'd promised. He'd keep Rory safe. No matter what.

Brody lifted his head and looked in vain through the sheets of water. But still, he couldn't see. He could only hope he was going in the right direction.

He dug deep and paddled harder, forcing the board through the water.

And then, through the howling wind and the pounding rain, he heard it. A shriek. It was close. It was the sound of a little girl.

Rory.

He had to make it. He had to get there in time.

Sarah couldn't take her eyes off the scene before her. The swim platform raft pitched and tipped precariously in the building storm. The little girls clung to the cold slippery wood, but for how long?

What were they doing out there? How had they gotten out there?

So many questions, but it wasn't the time to get any answers. Nor did they matter. The only thing that mattered was Brody getting to the platform safely and quickly and getting the girls.

The paddleboard he was on slammed up and down in the waves. His progress was laborious and made harder by the gusting winds.

Sarah wrapped her arms around her waist, clinging to herself tightly in an effort to force herself to stop shivering. Whatever cold she was feeling, it was nothing compared to what the girls were feeling. Or the type of bone-deep chill she'd never be able to warm up from if Brody didn't make it.

"Oh my God! Clara!" Audrey was next to her, screaming into the storm. Sarah hadn't noticed her arrive. "What are they doing out there?" She turned to Sarah, her face crumpled with fear and worry. "How did they get out there?" she demanded of Sarah. Mascara ran down her face, streaked by tears or rain or both.

Sarah was sure she looked the same.

Two mothers. So different, but so fundamentally the same when it came to the only thing that mattered.

Their daughters.

There were no answers, so Sarah took Audrey's hand in hers and squeezed tightly as they watched Brody make his way to the swim platform. "He'll get there," Sarah said, not sure whether she was speaking to Audrey or to herself. "He'll get there."

The other woman nodded but didn't take her eyes off the lake.

"He's almost there."

But Sarah could see he was having trouble. It must be impossible to see with the waves and the rain. He lifted his head up to check his distance and that's when it happened. A hard wave came up and rocked the platform violently. Clara slid on the slippery wood. Next to her, Audrey gasped and clutched Sarah's hand tighter as the raft pitched, sending Clara straight into Rory, knocking her into the water.

"No!"

Sarah broke away and ran until her feet were in the water. "Rory!"

"Sarah, no." Byron had appeared. He wrapped a towel around her shoulders and backed her up gently onto the sand. "He's got her. Brody's got her. It's okay. It's going to be okay."

But she didn't know whether she believed that. How could she? She'd lost her husband in that lake. And now…her daughter…in the middle of a storm. She wasn't a strong swimmer. She was in the water. In the lake. And Brody. *Oh God.* She squeezed her eyes shut, but only for a second. *Keep them safe, Josh,* she pleaded. *Please. Keep them safe. I can't lose them, too.*

"He's got her!" Byron yelled.

Her eyes flew open. She strained to see them through the hard rain, but it did in fact look like Brody had pulled Rory out of the lake. The paddleboard pitched wildly, but Rory was lying flat, the way Brody had a moment earlier. He was in the water now, with one hand on the board and one hand reaching out to Clara. She took it and he quickly pulled her onto the board as well.

"Oh thank God," Audrey cried. "They're going to be okay."

But Brody wasn't getting on the board with them. Sarah shook her head in disbelief. He had to get on the board. He couldn't swim in these conditions. *No.*

"It's going to be fine," Byron was saying. "He's on his way back."

And he was. Slowly. Brody was at the back of the board, hanging off, his upper body holding on and his legs kicking. The going was easier on the way back because of the direction of the wind, but still, the board slammed up and down violently.

Some parents who'd been standing by, watching, ran out into the water up to their waists, ready to receive the board and its precious cargo. As soon as Brody was close enough, Sarah watched him slide off the back and shove it as hard as he could. The paddleboard, and the girls, sailed smoothly through the water into the waiting hands of the parents who scooped them up and ran them to the shore.

The moment her daughter was in her arms, Sarah crumpled to the wet sand, sobbing.

Rory clung to her, shivering and sobbing. "I'm sorry, Mom. I'm so sorry."

"It's okay. It's okay." Sarah held her tight, unwilling to let go. "You're okay."

Rory started babbling incoherently about her experience,

her small voice muffled against Sarah's chest. "Cold and…the rain….slipped…Brody came and—"

"Brody!"

Sarah lifted her head and with Rory still clinging to her, she searched the water, trying to find the last spot where she'd seen him. Right before he'd shoved the paddleboard and the girls to safety. *Where was he? No. No. No.*

She could not lose him, too. She could not. *No!*

"Brody?" She whispered his name and she continued to search in vain. And when she still couldn't see him, she screamed. "Brody!" In her arms, Rory squirmed against her as she screamed again. "Brody! No!"

She fell to her knees and buried her face into Rory's wet hair, defeated and heartbroken. He'd promised her he'd keep Rory safe. A promise he'd kept. But he hadn't promised he'd come back to her.

Wrung out, with a barge of emotions slamming through her, she didn't hear her name the first time. Or the second.

"Sarah?"

Finally, she looked up and blinked. Once and then again. "Brody?"

He grinned down at her. "Who else—"

She didn't give him a chance to finish; she leapt to her feet and wrapped her arms around him, needing to feel him to believe it was really him. Sarah was vaguely aware that Rory was still sandwiched between them. But she didn't care if she hadn't explained anything to her daughter about their relationship yet. Or that she'd barely even figured it out herself. She didn't care about anything as she pressed her lips to his and kissed him hard—except that she had her entire family in her arms. Safe.

Chapter Seventeen

ON MONDAY MORNING, Faith's smile only got bigger and bigger as she looked over the proofs of the photos that Dan had sent over earlier that morning. They were perfect.

Even the pictures of Brody and Sarah, although stiff and forced at first because of whatever it was that was going on between them that day, were magical, too. The photographer had managed to catch the moments when their guards weren't up and they were being honest and genuine. And they were absolutely stunning.

Made even more special by the close call they'd all had the day before at the lake.

Faith had heard about it, just as everyone else in town had. Brody's efforts to save Rory and Clara in the middle of such an intense storm were being hailed as nothing short of heroic, and Faith could absolutely believe it. She couldn't even begin to imagine how Sarah would have coped if anything had happened to either Rory or Brody, not after everything she'd already been through. Everyone could see how much she loved that man—had for months—and judging by the stories she'd heard about the kiss she'd laid on him when he got out of the water, Sarah finally had realized it, too.

Faith selected a few of the images, attached them to an email, and composed a quick note.

I'm happy everyone is okay. Even happier that you two finally got past whatever was keeping you apart. I thought you might enjoy these.

XO ~Faith

She'd just sent the email when there was a knock at her front door. "Come in!" she hollered and a few moments later, Nicole appeared in her kitchen, holding a takeout tray of coffee.

"Thanks." Faith took the offered cup. "You didn't have to bring drinks. I could have…" Everyone knew she had many talents, but cooking of any kind, including making a simple palatable coffee, wasn't one of them. "I'm glad you could come by," she said instead. "I'm dying to show you these pictures."

She scooted her chair over to make room for Nicole, who tucked in to look at the computer screen with her.

Faith started to click and open the files. "I think you're really going to—"

"Holy…oh my…" Nicole's hand flew to her mouth and she shook her head as tears formed in her eyes.

She looked to Faith, who simply nodded. She knew her friend would be emotional looking at the photos of her and Amy.

They were absolutely stunning. But more than that was the emotion in every shot. The way they looked at each other, with so much love in their eyes, it would be clear to anyone how much love there was between the two women. They were absolutely some of the most beautiful photographs Faith had ever seen.

And they weren't even from a *real* wedding.

"They're pretty special, aren't they?"

Faith clicked her mouse and her favorite image of the couple appeared. They stood in front of the river, holding hands and looking into each other's eyes, completely oblivious of the photographer capturing every moment.

"I have to tell you, Nicole. I've seen quite a few weddings now, and dozens of couples during their photo shoots, and the two of you…it was different. The love that the two of you have for each other is something pretty special."

Nicole nodded. "It is." She looked at Faith with tears in her eyes. "It's like nothing I've ever experienced before. And it's funny you called this morning because ever since we took those photos, I've been thinking. And then with what happened to Brody and the girls at the lake yesterday…well…I've given it some thought. A lot actually. And Amy and I have been talking and…well…we don't want to wait anymore. We want to get married and—"

"Yes!"

Both women burst out laughing.

"Sorry," Faith said with a shake of her head. "I assumed you were asking me if you could get married at Ever After. But please don't feel like—"

"Oh my God. Yes. That's exactly what we were asking. But I know how busy you are and—"

"We'll make it happen." Faith mentally scanned her appointment book. They were pretty full up, but if the ladies were willing to choose a date other than the traditional Saturday, they could absolutely make it happen. And she knew without a doubt that she'd bend over backward for the two of them.

So much had shifted within her since she'd moved back to Glacier Falls. Hope would laugh if she could see her now, excited to squeeze yet another wedding into the schedule because she believed so much in the couple and their love.

It certainly was a complete one-eighty, that was for sure. But Faith no longer cared. Something in her was definitely starting to melt.

"Life's too short," Nicole said with a huge grin. "And when you find the one who makes you feel all the things and you can't imagine even one day without, well…what's the point in waiting? You know what I mean?"

Faith let her eyes drift to the window and across the yard, where Logan was just getting out of his truck. He stretched and turned to look straight at the house. Her stomach did a flip at the sight of him, the way it always seemed to these days.

Did Logan make her feel *all the things*? Maybe.

Could she imagine going even one day without him? That wasn't as easy to answer. He'd been part of her life for so long, and they'd spent every day all summer together. And yes, she looked forward to seeing him. And she expected to see him every day. What would it feel like if he wasn't there? She couldn't answer that.

But she'd resisted Logan for so long that it was almost a habit to do it. If asked, Faith couldn't even be sure what she'd say was her reason for keeping him at arms' length.

She'd had a reason once. *What was it?*

She shook her head in response to her friend as she watched Logan head into the barn. "Honestly? I'm not sure if I do know."

Faith took a minute to shake off the unsettled feeling that she'd been getting more and more when it came to Logan. She wouldn't be able to ignore it forever, that much she knew, but she'd try to push it off a little longer.

"So," Faith refocused on her friend. "Tell me how I can help you and Amy?"

Chapter Eighteen

A MOAN ESCAPED Sarah's lips as Brody's hands traced the length of her body, from her shoulder to the curve of her hip. His touch was like nothing she'd ever experienced before. Still half asleep, she wiggled backward to press herself into him. His hard length pressed up against her back and her body responded instantly, moisture pooling between her legs despite her half-asleep state.

It was Brody's turn to groan. He pulled her closer and kissed the back of her neck as he swept her hair out of the way. "Good morning, beautiful."

"Mmmm." Talking wasn't high on her priority list for morning activities.

Thankfully, it didn't take long for Brody to get the message. A moment later, he had his arm around her, cupping her breast as he slid into her wet heat from behind.

They moved together slowly, a perfect fit.

She gasped as Brody's hand reached around and moved between her legs. With the multiple sensations, it didn't take long for the pressure to build inside her until finally Sarah's orgasm flowed through her like a warm wave that touched every part of her. Seconds later, while she was still vibrating, Brody took his own release as he held her tight, as if she might slip away.

He needn't have worried. She wasn't going anywhere.

"It certainly is a good morning." Brody chuckled as he turned and propped himself up on pillows so she could snuggle on his chest.

She inhaled his scent and let it fill her. *Why had she tried to push him away?*

She couldn't even make sense of how she was feeling so conflicted only a few short days ago because, in that moment, with him in her bed, and her safe in his arms, Sarah couldn't imagine them being any other way.

"You're quiet this morning."

She lifted her head and looked into his eyes. "I'm just enjoying you here."

"Here in your bed, here? Or here *here?*"

She grinned. "Both."

It had been two days since the *incident* at the lake. It still set her heart racing when she thought about that afternoon and the fear that had gripped her when she thought she'd lost him.

It was too much. The thought that she might never see him again. That she might have lost him the same way that she'd lost Josh.

No. Not the same at all.

Still...the moment she'd seen him again, she'd grabbed hold of him, and she'd barely let go since.

Brody kissed her on the forehead. "I'm enjoying being here, too."

After making sure Rory and Clara—and of course Brody —were okay after their terrifying ordeal, the only thing Sarah had wanted to do was be at home. And that's exactly where they'd been ever since. Sarah had called in some sick days, and Brody had Amy cover for him at the restaurant, and the three of them had holed up inside—watching movies, eating pizza, playing board games—and when Rory went to bed, the two of them would sneak down the hall to her bedroom and make love. It had been the perfect few days.

No stress. No worry. No real life. And as much as Sarah would have been content keeping it that way forever, she knew it wasn't realistic. They would have to face the world soon enough.

But she'd be ready for it.

Sarah was done avoiding life and the hard things.

With a sigh, she sat up and pulled the sheet up to cover her breasts.

"Uh-oh." Brody scooted backward against the headboard. "That doesn't look like a face that's enjoying much of anything."

His tone was teasing and light, but Sarah saw the worry flash in his eyes at the shift in her expression.

"Oh no." She smiled as she reached out for his hand. "I am very much enjoying you here, but I also think it's probably time we talk."

"I don't know if I like the sound of that."

She didn't blame him for being trepidatious; she hadn't exactly been an easy person to get close to. But she was hoping to change all of that once and for all.

"Time for a good talk," she amended. "As much as I'd like to ignore real life for a while longer, I don't think that's going to be possible. I mean, Rory's going to ask a question or two soon. The fact that she hasn't yet is kind of a miracle." She laughed. "I think she just likes having you around."

"As much as her mother?" Brody winked and wrapped his fingers between hers so he could pull her a little closer.

Sarah laughed. It was so easy to be with Brody. And it felt so good. But the laughter died on her lips as she remembered what it had felt like to stand on the shore and not see him there. To think she'd lost him. *Could she risk her heart like that again?* Only different this time, because what she felt for Brody was so completely different than what she'd felt for Josh.

She squeezed her eyes shut. It wasn't long ago that she wasn't sure if she could. *But now…*

"I thought I lost you," she said as she reopened her eyes. "When I couldn't see you there it was—"

"It's okay."

"No." She shook her head. "It's not okay, because I need you to know this, Brody." He nodded and she continued. "I was so scared. Of course I was terrified that I'd lost you. But also, I was afraid that we'd missed our chance. That we'd never know how we could be together or what we could have had. And all because I was too frozen to let you in." A tear streaked down her cheek but she didn't wipe it away. "I was wrong to push you away for so long, Brody. And I hate that it took a close call for me to understand that properly, but…it's all just so clear now. You make me feel things I've never felt before. *Never.* I can feel the way you love me, and I need you to know…" She took a deep breath. "I said it before, and I'll say it again and again and again. It may have taken awhile for me to figure it all out, but I love you, Brody. And I want this…if you still want it."

Having said everything she'd needed to say for way too long, Sarah released a breath and waited.

But Brody didn't keep her waiting long. He pulled her across the small distance on the bed separating them and kissed her hard. "Damn, woman, but I've been waiting for you to say those words for far too long. Of course I want this. You… Rory…all of it, because I am so crazy in love with you. And I'm pretty sure I've been in love with you from the moment I met you."

More tears spilled down Sarah's face, but these were all

tears of happiness. "I think that now that I have you here, I might not let you go."

He kissed her and pulled her tighter. "I'm totally good with that. I can't actually imagine being anywhere else than right here with you."

"Thank you for being so patient with me and all my crazy."

"Baby, I'll take your crazy any day, all day."

"Oh, you ain't seen nothing yet."

He wrapped his arms around her and pressed her back into the bed. He hovered over her and pressed kisses all over her face. "I can't wait to—"

A knock on the door sent Brody flying off her.

Rory!

They hadn't really explained their relationship to Rory yet. But at the same time, they hadn't tried to hide their affection for each other either. Everything had just happened as a natural evolution, and Rory had seemed to accept it. He'd always spent a lot of time with them, but the hugs and kisses were new. As was the discovery of finding her coach in her mom's bed.

Shit.

Sarah tugged the covers back over her bare chest but before she could react further, the door opened and Rory ran into the room. She jumped on the bed between them and looked at them both in turn. Sarah braced herself for the question that was inevitable. That would be so hard to explain.

She tensed, but when Rory asked, "Can we have pancakes for breakfast?" her tension evaporated and she burst into laughter.

"I think they're ready to flip," Brody told Rory, who was perched on a chair next to the stove, an apron tied around her waist and a spatula in her hand, watching the pancakes on the griddle intently. "When they get these little bubbles on them, they're ready," Brody explained. "Do you want to do it?"

Rory nodded seriously, so Brody gave her a quick explanation and stood back while she shoved the spatula under a pancake before slamming it down into the pan. He couldn't help but laugh. "Not bad for a first effort. Next time, just try it a little more gently, okay?"

She tried again, and after a few flips, actually turned out to be pretty good at it.

"Nice work, kiddo."

Being with Rory and Sarah in this way was so easy and it felt so right. As did waking up with Sarah's naked body pressed up against his for the last few mornings. That felt *very* right. He was going to have a very hard time moving back into his own little house with the big empty bed.

In fact, everything felt empty about his house. Without Rory and Sarah in it, it wasn't much of a home. He glanced over at Sarah, who sat at the kitchen table with a cup of coffee. She was alternating between watching the two of them cook and checking out her social media feeds on her tablet. As if she sensed him watching her, she looked up from her tablet and grinned at him. He blew her a kiss and went back to supervising the pancake flipping.

A few minutes later, Rory carried a plate full of piping-hot pancakes to the table and breakfast was ready.

It wasn't until after they'd eaten, and Sarah had sent Rory to go change and she was gathering up the dishes, that she slid her tablet toward Brody. "Check this out. Faith is going to lose her mind."

Brody clicked on the tablet and saw what Sarah had been referring to. It was a photo from their photo shoot the week before, but it wasn't a picture of Brody and Sarah like the ones Faith had sent over the day before. Instead, it was a close-up of

Faith and Logan in a very intense, passionate embrace that had obviously been part of Logan's *demonstration* kiss.

"What is this?" Brody looked up with wide eyes and shook his head before looking back to the screen and scrolling down to the article.

"Faith said something about the photographer giving her a deal if he could use a few of the pictures in a freelance article about weddings he had commissioned. But…"

"This isn't a wedding picture."

Sarah laughed. "Nope. And read the article."

Brody scanned down. The headline read, *"Twins find their own Ever After in love-inspired location."* He quickly scanned the article, which was actually a great advertisement piece about Ever After and both Faith and Hope, who ran it. The only problem was, Faith hadn't found love the way the article described it.

"It's pretty great, don't you think?" Sarah didn't even bother hiding her glee at the misinformation, and Brody could see why.

Faith was going to freak out. Although it was clear to anyone who saw them together that there was something between them, Faith behaved as if Logan were a giant pain in her ass and had been adamantly denying that she had any feelings for him at all. And from what Brody heard around town, it had been like that since they were in high school.

"Oh man," Brody agreed. "You're right. Faith is going to freak out, and Logan is going to love it." He took a few minutes and read the rest of the article while he finished his coffee. When he took the cup to the sink, he wrapped his arms around Sarah and kissed her on the cheek. "Why don't you go have a shower and get ready for the day while I finish up in here?"

They'd both still taken the day off work, but they'd made the decision to actually leave the house, grab some lunch at the restaurant, and maybe even rent some bikes from the Hub. But first, Brody had other plans.

The moment he heard the water running in the shower, as much as he would have liked to join her, Brody sprang into action. He hadn't spent much time planning or really, anything at all. But he'd made the decision to follow his heart. And he was going to need Rory's help.

By the time Sarah emerged from the bathroom, her hair still wet and hanging down her shoulders, they were ready. Brody peeked around the corner of the kitchen into the living room where he'd left the note.

He watched as Sarah picked it up.

There's a seat and a treat waiting for you outside.

She smiled and looked around.

Brody ducked back into the kitchen before she could see him. A moment later, he heard the patio door open and he looked down at Rory, who was grinning broadly. "Ready?"

She nodded. "Tell me what to say again."

Brody chuckled and bent down so he could look her in the eye. "I want you to take this to your mom." He handed her the tray that held a single daisy he'd picked from her front garden. "Ask her to put it in her hair and close her eyes."

Rory giggled.

"Can you do that?"

She nodded and looked affronted. "Duh. Of course."

"I know you can," Brody added quickly. "And then, once her eyes are closed, and make sure she keeps them closed, hit the Play button on my phone." He handed her his cell phone, which she tucked into her pocket with a serious nod. "Got it?"

"Got it, Coach." She turned to get to her task, but stopped and looked at him before going. "Does this mean you're going to be around more?"

Brody grinned. "I sure hope so. Is that okay?"

Rory nodded seriously. "It's about time."

If he hadn't been so nervous, he would have laughed. But instead, Brody closed his eyes and took a deep breath. He'd spent too long not listening to his heart. It was time for things to change.

A few moments later, the music started and Brody exhaled slowly. It was time.

He walked outside. Maybe it was the heightened emotion of the moment, but his breath caught in his throat at the sight of Sarah, her hair hanging wet down her back, the daisy tucked simply and beautifully behind her ear. She sat up straight in the chair with a small smile on her lips, waiting for whatever was going to happen next.

He shoved his nerves down, crossed the deck, and took her hand in his. "May I have this dance?"

The song was a popular one on the radio music stations over the last few months, and every single time that it played, he thought of Sarah. It was perfect.

She took his hand and opened her eyes, and he pulled her close in his arms and started swaying her around the deck. They'd danced together once before, at Katie and Damon's wedding reception, but it was a faster two-step and not the emotion-packed slow song. Never mind how things had shifted between them since then.

"What's going on?" Her eyes sparkled with question, but she went with it. A fact he was grateful for.

Brody spun her out before pulling her close again. "I wanted a special moment with you."

She seemed to like the answer and tucked her head under his chin as they moved together. The song floated in the air.

He turned her slowly. "I hope by now, after everything, you know exactly how I feel about you, Sarah."

She lifted her head a little to look him in the eyes.

"I am completely head over heels in love with you, and I can't imagine another day without waking up with you in my arms. I'm ready to experience everything we can have together, and I hope like hell you are, too."

The song washed over them as Brody dipped her low in his arms. Shocked, her lips formed an *O*, but a second later when he pulled her back up and dropped to one knee, Sarah's hands flew up to cover her mouth.

"Sarah Lewis, will you make me the happiest man in the world and marry me?"

Her entire body shook with the surprise as he held out his grandmother's ruby ring, but he waited for his words to register and when they finally did, she nodded.

"Yes," she said, the word muffled through her hands. "Yes! This is the craziest thing." She laughed. "But, yes. A million times, yes!"

From behind them, Rory shrieked.

Brody slid the ring onto her hand, a perfect fit, and jumped to his feet in time to catch Rory and lift her into his arms so they could share an embrace as a new family unit.

"It's about time," Rory said, repeating her comment from earlier.

Sarah's gaze locked onto his. An unshed tear glistened in her eyes. "It *is* about time, isn't it? For so many reasons."

Unable to wait a moment longer, Brody closed the distance between them, and kissed his new fiancée.

"Ew!" Rory wiggled out of his arms and jumped down.

He shrugged at her response and once more pulled Sarah close and kissed her properly.

Chapter Nineteen

"THERE'S no way you think this is funny!" Faith paced back and forth in her kitchen. Her sister's face filled the screen on her laptop that was perched on the counter. And although Hope was usually identical to Faith, the smile on her sister's face clearly didn't match the frown on her own. "Because this is *not* funny. Not even a little bit."

It hadn't taken long for the article that *featured* the love stories of the Turner twins to make its way to Hope and Levi on their travels. And even less time for them to video call Faith to see what it was they'd missed.

"It's not that I think it's funny," Hope said, trying and failing to hide her amusement. "I think it's wonderful. You and Logan...we all knew——"

"You know it's bullshit." She spun on her toe and faced her sister. "Logan and I are not....well, we're not anything." She pointed at the screen. "And you know that."

Hope raised her eyebrows and Faith had to fight the urge to slam the computer lid down. The article had her seriously fired up. How Dan Drummond had extrapolated that she and Logan were happily coupled up was beyond her.

Was it?

They said a picture was worth a thousand words, and the photo that accompanied the article was…well, it was…

"I don't know," Hope was saying. "It sure looks like the two of you are *something*. I haven't seen a kiss like that in a very long time. Especially not between two people who claim they don't have feelings for each other. But if you say that—"

"I do say that!" Faith knew she was protesting too much. Especially because when she saw the photo, she'd been completely mesmerized. It really did look as if they were madly, deeply in love. And just looking at the image brought back all the feelings of that moment. Logan's lips on hers. His tongue twisted up with hers. His body pressed up against hers so she could feel every inch of him and how badly he wanted her.

Damn.

"Whatever you say, sis." Hope laughed. "Honestly, when are you going to get over all this nonsense about not believing in love? It's getting a little old. Hasn't running Ever After changed your mind about things at all?"

Faith pulled up a chair and sat down backward, facing the screen and her sister. She sighed hard. *Had it changed her mind? Was it all nonsense?*

The conversation she'd overheard her parents having definitely hadn't been nonsense. But maybe she'd been wrong all this time. After all, her parents had fought, certainly. But they'd still loved each other, hadn't they? At the time she hadn't thought so. Faith's teenage self had been so sure that they'd been putting on a front for their friends and neighbors. But maybe she'd been wrong. Maybe their argument, no matter how serious it had been, hadn't been the destruction of them.

She had a lot to think about.

"So," Hope prompted. "Remember when you said you

were going to tell me why you have such crazy ideas about love anyway? It's way past time. Spill."

Faith stared at her twin on the screen. They were thousands of miles apart, but in so many ways it felt as if she were right there in the room with her. Hope's face was slightly rounder than it had been before she'd left. Whether that was from all the good food they'd had traveling or the early stages of pregnancy, she didn't know. Either way, it looked good on her, because she looked incredibly happy.

"Did I tell you about the wedding we're having next week?" Faith changed the subject, unwilling to upset her sister with the truth. "I swear, I'm going to start specializing in last-minute weddings. It's beginning to become a bit of a trend around here."

Hope laughed, but Faith could tell she wasn't going to let it go so easily this time. "Who is it?"

Faith straightened up in her chair. "Nicole Lewis. Remember Josh's sister? Sarah's sister-in-law. Oh, remind me to tell you about Sarah and Brody, too."

"Nicole?" Hope looked genuinely shocked. "Of course I remember her. You forget I never moved away. And yes, don't forget to tell me about Sarah and Brody, but only if it's good news," she added. "Who is Nicole marrying? I always thought she was…"

"Gay?" Faith finished for her. "She is. And she has met the love of her life. Her name is Amy." For the next few minutes, Faith filled her sister in on all the details of Nicole and Amy and they both agreed that it was fantastic. There had been a bit of pushback in town from some of the less liberal townspeople when it came to same-sex marriage, but neither Faith nor Hope cared what they thought because at the end of the day, anyone who was as in love, regardless of gender, race, or… well, anything, really…deserved to celebrate that love. And

Ever After Ranch was proud to host any celebration of love and dedication.

When they were finished talking about the upcoming weddings on the schedule, Faith did her sisterly duty and filled her in on Sarah and Brody, who'd *finally* gotten over themselves and discovered that not only were they desperately in love with each other, they had been for a very long time. The story of their engagement was one of the sweetest stories, and both Faith and Hope agreed that they couldn't wait to plan that wedding when the time came.

"I do have a bit more news for you," Hope added before they disconnected. The smile fell off her face. "It looks like we have to cut our trip short and come home next week."

Of all the things that Faith had been expecting, it hadn't been that. "Is everything okay?"

Hope nodded. "My blood pressure is a little high and the doctors want me closer. Mostly as a precaution. But it looks like I get to look forward to a whole lot of bed rest, so you're still going to be running things for a while, if that's okay?"

"Of course it's okay." Faith leaned forward. "But you're okay? You're sure? Everything is all right?"

"Honestly, I'm fine. But I'm not supposed to have any stress." She laughed. "So you and Levi can wait on me hand and foot, okay?"

Faith nodded. She'd do whatever it took to keep her sister and her unborn baby safe.

They discussed the details of their arrival home and said their good-byes.

Before Faith headed out to the barn and Logan, who would no doubt be arriving soon and want to make a big deal about their featured article, she tidied up the kitchen and gathered up the large manila envelope she'd found in a box of her parents' old files.

She'd meant it when she'd said that she'd do anything to

keep Hope and her baby safe. No stress? No problem. But that meant it wouldn't be anytime soon that she told Hope about that argument she'd overheard all those years ago, and the envelope that held the details of the subject of that argument.

The child their mother had given up for adoption before her parents were married.

No.

Faith would keep that particular detail to herself a little while longer.

She tucked the envelope into the cupboard over the fridge. She'd deal with it later.

Much later.

Chapter Twenty

ALMOST TWO WEEKS after it was decided, with no official engagement, Nicole and Amy tied the knot in a small and intimate ceremony tucked into the trees at the back of the Ever After Ranch property. With only about a dozen people in attendance, the couple was surrounded by love.

Sarah cried when they exchanged their heartfelt vows that they wrote themselves, and she wasn't the only one. Even Brody, who had his arm wrapped tightly around Sarah, dabbed at his eyes once or twice.

When the officiant declared them legally married, everyone in attendance tossed flower petals over their heads and instead of running off, they stayed and hugged each guest in turn.

"That was absolutely beautiful," Sarah gushed as she squeezed her sister-in-law in a tight hug. "I really couldn't be happier for the two of you. Love like yours is a rare thing."

Nicole couldn't wipe the smile off her face. "It seems like maybe you've found some of that rare stuff yourself." She winked.

Sarah laughed. She didn't want to steal any of the limelight from the brides, but she absolutely agreed. She had definitely found the *rare stuff* with Brody, and she couldn't wait until it was their turn to exchange vows, too. Although they hadn't planned anything concrete. They had time.

"I'm pretty happy," she admitted.

"Good." Nicole kissed her on the cheek. "You, more than anyone else, deserve it. You know I loved my brother, but…"

Her eyes took on a faraway look and instantly Sarah felt guilty. There shouldn't be any sad feelings on such a happy day.

"Nicole, don't—"

"No." She stopped her. "It's okay. I need to say this and I can't think of a better time." She smiled again to prove to Sarah she was fine. "I loved Josh very much and I know how much he loved you and Rory, but this…" She gestured to Brody, who was busy congratulating Amy and not paying attention to them. "This is special. It's different. It's everything it should be. I never said anything when you were with Josh because it wasn't my place, but—"

"It's okay." Sarah interrupted her with a hug. "I know exactly what you're saying. Thank you."

"I just want you to be happy and have everything."

It was typical Nicole, to be thinking about someone else on her special day. Sarah squeezed her tight.

"And I need you to know that what happened to Josh, it wasn't your fault."

Sarah pulled back suddenly and looked at her sister-in-law with a question on her face.

"We always knew," she said, referring to her and her parents. "He wasn't in the lake that day to save anyone."

Sarah's mouth had fallen open completely. She shook her head in disbelief. "Nicole, I—"

"There is no need to apologize. I know it was a mistake and you let us all think that's why he was in the lake that day. You did what you did to protect his memory. It wasn't malicious. You did what you felt was best. We knew that. We always did."

Sarah had started crying again. For a woman who'd hardly cried in years, she was sure doing a lot of it lately.

"But we always knew." Nicole smiled kindly. "And it's okay. Really."

"Oh, Nicole." Once again, Sarah pulled her in for a tight hug. "I'm so sorry and I just...I love you so much. Josh would be so proud of you today."

"Can I hug Auntie Nicole now?"

Rory had appeared next to them and stood with her arms crossed over her purple dress, looking very impatient with the proceedings.

"Of course, pretty girl." Nicole bent down and swept Rory into a hug.

Sarah took a moment to compose herself. She had no idea that people knew the truth about Josh. But then again, why wouldn't they? When the reporter had gotten the details wrong, she hadn't bothered to correct anyone. It didn't matter and ultimately it felt better if that's what everyone thought. Of course, she hadn't been thinking straight in that moment. It had been a mistake. But apparently one that wasn't irreversible. And it also made sense of the conversation she'd had earlier with Josh's parents, who'd hugged her and congratulated her on her new engagement.

She'd been worried about how they would take the news of her moving on, but just like everyone else, they seemed to be thrilled by it. And when Mrs. Lewis looked her in the eye and told her that Josh, too, would be happy for her, it had meant the world to her. Now, knowing that they had known all along the truth about Josh's swim that day, and had supported her in her story, filled her with love and compassion for her in-laws. She owed them an extra hug and a huge apology for the way she handled everything. But something told her they'd be okay with it, the same way their daughter had been.

The crowd had spread out a little as the small number of guests broke off to take pictures and chat. Across the clearing, Brody appeared to be in an in-depth conversation with her father. Both of them were smiling, which Sarah took as a good sign, because now that they'd finally worked through every-thing, Brody wasn't going anywhere. In fact, he'd already given up his small rental and had moved in with her and Rory, pretty much as soon as they could manage it. And with the financial issues with Birchwood—problems she hadn't even known he was having—all sorted out because of the increased amount of weddings and take-away lunches Brody had secured, it looked as if their future together would be solid.

Sarah grinned as she made her way over to her father and fiancé. She threaded her arm through Brody's and leaned against his shoulder. "You two look pretty intense."

"Not at all." Brody bent to put a kiss on the top of her head. "I was just having a nice talk with your dad."

Ed jumped in. "I was commending your young man for his heroic actions at the lake and saving my favorite girl." He grinned. "Well, one of my favorite girls."

"Thanks, Dad." Sarah shook her head but there was a grin on her face.

"I also wanted to properly congratulate the two of you on your engagement." Her father straightened his spine and cleared his voice, clearly uncomfortable with the show of emotion. "I know I wasn't sure about…well…I may not have been totally supportive of…"

"It's okay, Dad."

"No." Ed shook his head. "It's not. I don't think it was fair of me to compare myself with you. And seeing the two of you together and the love you clearly have for each other, well…" He swallowed hard. "It's clear to anyone who looks at you that the two of you share something special. And I'm eternally thankful that you found each other."

"I appreciate you saying that, Mr. Walker."

He waved away Brody's formality. "Ed. Call me Ed." He wiped his hands together. "Now what do you say we go celebrate the couple of the hour?"

Before he could make his leave, Sarah threw her arms around her dad and squeezed. "Thank you, Dad," she whispered into his ear. "I love you."

"I love you too, kiddo." He kissed her on the cheek. "Be happy. That's all I've ever wanted for you."

She watched as he walked away before turning to Brody and kissing him squarely on the lips.

"Not that I'm complaining," he said with a laugh when she pulled away. "But what was that for?"

She looked him straight in the eye, and with more love and peace in her heart than she could have possibly imagined, she said, "For being my happy ever after."

Chapter Twenty-One

IT HAD TURNED out to be a beautiful and simple wedding, and despite the lack of pomp and circumstance, it may have ended up being Faith's favorite to date. After the ceremony, the small group of guests made their way back to the barn for appetizers and a few drinks. No cake to cut. No speeches except for a toast given by the fathers of each bride. And no dance, except for one shared by the happy couple while everyone held hands in a circle around them.

It really was all absolutely perfect for them.

Only a few guests still lingered, but Faith had retreated to a quiet corner of the barn to check her voicemail. There was only one message. And it was quite clear. There was no disputing the request. Still, she hit the button that would replay the message for the third time and listened to it again, still unable to believe her ears.

Ms. Turner.

This is Stephanie Starz. I wanted to reach out personally because I read the article on Weddings Weekly and I was so impressed. As you might have heard, I'm engaged to be married.

Everyone had heard! Stephanie Starz was one of the hottest and most in-demand movie stars in Hollywood. She hailed from a small Canadian town no one had heard of, which only made her a bigger star in Canada, and she had recently had a very public engagement to Dax Combs, an equally big, albeit maybe not *quite* as big, movie star. Everyone knew about it.

I've been absolutely obsessed with planning the perfect wedding but I couldn't find the right place. Until now! Ever After Ranch looks absolutely perfect for what we want and it's even better because it's obviously a lucky location.

Lucky? What the…

If both you and your sister can find your Prince Charming and fall in love when the odds are against you, that's exactly the type of place I want to get married at and the people I want planning it. Talk about lucky twins.

Seriously?

Please reach out to my assistant so we can set up a time to come and visit. And I can't wait to meet you and your man. I think we'll all get along famously.

Nope. The message was still the same the third time she played it. What the actual fuck? Hollywood's biggest couple wanted to get married at Ever After? With the *lucky twins* organizing? And Hope was going to lose her mind. It was crazy. Also…it wasn't going to happen.

"Was that Stephanie Starz? On the phone?"

Faith whipped her head up to see Logan leaning against a wooden beam, watching her with a sly grin. Her stomach did a flip and her heart raced. He looked good. *Really* good. And try as she might, she couldn't seem to stop looking at him without thinking about that kiss or the way it had made her feel. Like she wanted to rip his clothes off and push him into the shrubs. It didn't help that the picture of that very kiss seemed to be everywhere these days.

She tried to push the image from her head. "It was." She nodded as casually as she could, as if it were perfectly normal for Hollywood's biggest celebrity to call her out of the blue and want to meet her.

"She wants to have her wedding here?" Logan walked closer.

Damn. She wished he wouldn't do that.

"At Ever After?"

Faith nodded.

"That's huge."

"It's not going to happen." She stood up from the bench, feeling at a disadvantage somehow with him standing. "She thinks we're together."

Logan laughed. "Everyone thinks we're together."

"No!" Faith swallowed hard. "No one thinks we're together." She tried to sound calmer than she felt. "At least, no one who knows us thinks we're together."

He took another step closer until he was only inches away. He put his hand on the wall behind her and leaned in.

She was sure he was going to kiss her again, and she couldn't seem to decide whether she wanted him to or not. Her body and her brain were in a full-out war when it came to Logan Langdon.

"What would it hurt to pretend?" His voice dripped with heat. "I mean, if it landed us the biggest wedding of the year, why not?"

Why not? Why not? She could think of a million reasons *why not.* At least, she thought she could. At that moment, she couldn't seem to think of any except...

"I mean, if you think you can handle all this." He laughed

and pushed back so there was a bit of distance between them again.

And there it was. The reason she wouldn't be pretending anything that involved Logan. *Because he was Logan. And he made her crazy.*

"I can handle it, all right." She swallowed hard and smoothed her hair back. "That's not the question here."

"Then what is?"

Dammit.

"We're not going to pretend to be a couple like Damon and Katie did." She shook her head and crossed her arms. "Not for a job."

"It's not just any job," he countered. "Besides, it wouldn't be like Damon and Katie. That was different because they actually have always been madly in love with each other and we—"

"Haven't," she finished for him, doing her best to hide the unexpected sting his words had. It didn't make any sense for her to be affected by his words, anyway. After all, he'd driven her crazy their entire life. He'd done nothing but tease her and poke fun at her when they were kids. When they were old enough, he seemed to take some sort of extra-special glee in flaunting his ridiculously attractive self at her and his teasing took on a whole new level. But *love?* Nope. No way.

"Whatever." He waved his hand and started to turn away before facing her again. "It's a bad idea anyway."

"What?" Her spine stiffened. "Why?"

He took a step toward her again.

She inhaled sharply, hating herself for being so affected by him.

"Because you can't do it anyway. You're a terrible actress. You'd never be able to pull it off."

"Bullshit!"

"What?" His lips twisted up into a dangerously sexy grin. "You think you can pull it off?"

"I know I can." She cocked her head. "I don't think *you* could. No way you have it in you to act like a loved-up boyfriend type. That's not your style."

Something flashed in his eyes and he took a deep breath before letting it out slowly. "You're on."

"On?"

"Yeah. I'll bet you I can do it." He widened his stance. "In fact, I'll bet you that I can do it, but you can't. I'll even make it a bet worth your while."

Alarm bells rang in the back of her head, but Faith was never one to back down from a dare, and definitely not a bet. "How's that?"

"If you can outlast me and pull off the wedding of the century while pretending to be desperately in love with me, I'll back off."

"You'll back off?"

"I'll leave." He shrugged, as though it were no big deal. "I'll go back to running my own ranch and leave you alone. You know exactly what I mean."

She did. And now that she was faced with it, Faith could no longer be sure that she wanted him to back off. But her stubbornness won out. "And if you win?" She shook her head quickly. "Not that you will."

"No," he mocked her. "Of course not." She glared at him, and he laughed. "If I win, and you can't hack it…" He pretended to think about it for a minute. "Then I get you for a whole night."

Her entire body flashed with heat, moisture pooling instantly between her legs. "Pardon me? There's no way I'm betting a night of sex."

"Who said anything about sex?" He looked taken aback,

but then he winked. "At least, not as my prize." Logan bit his bottom lip a little and gave her a look full of promise.

The details of which, more than anything else at that moment, she wanted to find out.

"Do we have a bet?"

Faith's body was on fire, the alarm bells clanging at full volume. Making a deal with the devil would not end well. She knew she should walk away. She was a grownup. She could say no. She could turn around and— "Deal." She heard herself speak, and as if she were experiencing an out-of-body moment, she saw her offer her hand to shake on it.

"Oh no." Logan took her hand in his and pulled her toward him until she was pressed up against the length of him. "A bet like this needs to be sealed with a kiss."

And before she could protest, his lips were on hers and she was melting into the hottest kiss she'd ever experienced. It only lasted a second before Logan pulled away and touched her lips gently with one finger.

"I'll see you soon."

He walked away, leaving her standing in the darkened corner, unable to fully make sense of what had just happened. Her fingers floated up to her lips that were still on fire. Her heart raced and before her legs gave out from under her, Faith sat down hard on the chair, dropped her head in her hands, and took a deep breath.

She was so screwed.

And worse—she couldn't decide whether that was a good thing or not.

I hope you enjoyed Sarah and Brody's story of healing hurts and hearts. There is a lot more love in store and it's finally time for Faith to find her happily

ever after...or does she? Find out in *Fighting Happily Ever After*. Read on for a special sneak peek!

Don't forget to join my mailing list where you'll be the first to hear about new stories, sales and promotions and giveaways!
You can join me here —>
https://elenaaitken.com/newsletter/

Fighting Happily Ever After

Please enjoy this excerpt from the fourth in the Ever After Series—*Fighting Happily Ever After*

There was so much to do, and as was always the case, not enough time to get any of it done. Faith Turner downed the last of her cup of coffee and moved to refill it but the pot was empty. *Empty.* She'd drank an entire pot of coffee. Bad coffee at that. She was definitely not known for her culinary skills, and somehow that extended to the simple act of making coffee.

Still, desperate times called for desperate measures and she was certainly desperate to stay awake. At least until she could cross some things off her to-do list. There was still a full month left in prime wedding season, and August was looking more and more like it would be a very full month for celebrations at Ever After Ranch, the wedding venue Faith now co-owned with her identical twin sister, Hope.

With Hope and her fiancé Levi on what was supposed to be a world traveling honeymoon trip, the weddings had all fallen to Faith to plan *and* execute. A huge task for most, but especially for a woman who quite vocally and adamantly declared that the whole idea of love was bullshit. A wedding planner who didn't believe in love! Not even the most optimistic residents of Glacier Falls actually thought that Faith would be able to make a go of it. To be fair, neither did Faith herself.

Although, if she was asked—at least by a close friend—Faith might actually admit that her feelings on the matter were starting to change.

How could they not?

She'd witnessed more demonstrations of true love in the last few months at the ranch than she had in her entire life leading up to being a reluctant wedding planner. Maybe there was something to it after all?

The thought made her smile as she yanked the freshly washed sheets out of the dryer and headed up to the second floor of her childhood home. Her sister was coming home from her honeymoon much earlier than planned. Faith was not excited that the only reason Hope and Levi were coming home earlier than planned from their honeymoon trip was because of Hope's health. But still, it would be good to have her home. Especially since she was pregnant.

Never mind the cancer diagnosis that Hope had received right before quickly getting married and jetting off on an around the world adventure where she got knocked up.

No matter what the circumstances, it would be good to have her close again. Their arrival was still a few days away, but if she didn't get their room made up now, it wouldn't happen. The next few days were going to be packed. There'd be little time for making beds, let alone sleeping. With one last wistful thought toward her empty coffee pot, Faith made quick work of the bed and headed back to her own room, stripping her clothes off and scattering them on the floor as she went.

She wasn't a messy person as a general rule, and her lowered standards were going to have to be picked up again soon with Hope and Levi moving in, but at least for a few more days she'd have the place to herself.

Faith let the hot shower water steam up in her attached bathroom before stepping inside and closing the glass door behind her. It felt good to let the water melt the tension from her shoulder muscles and she dropped her head back into the stream with a satisfied sigh.

She had a huge meeting later this morning with probably the biggest client Ever After ranch had ever seen. Stephanie Starz was the hottest celebrity in Hollywood and if she wanted to get married at the ranch, well, Faith was going to make sure she pulled it off and give Stephanie the wedding of her dreams. Despite the minor detail that she was deeply in over her head.

She should be preparing. Going over her notes one last time about the latest movies Stephanie had been in and the little Canadian town she herself had grown up in so Faith could relate it to Glacier Falls and why it was the perfect place for her to get married. In fact, she probably didn't have time to really enjoy the shower or dilly dally at all. But the hot water felt so good that she allowed herself the luxury of a few more minutes before working the shampoo into her long blond locks.

She closed her eyes and once more tipped her hair back, letting the hot water soothe her. A groan escaped her lips as the sudsy water washed out and down the drain. *How was it that a simple shower could feel so damn good?*

"I wish my showers were so satisfying."

What the—

Faith's head shot up, but with soap in her eyes, she wiped at them trying to see the owner of the voice. Not that she needed to. She knew exactly who had just walked into her *bathroom!*

"What the fuck, Logan?" Faith screamed and tried in vain to cover her body. Although the steamy glass door was probably providing some privacy. "I'm in the *shower!*"

"Oh, don't worry," came his reply. "I can see that."

She didn't have to see his eyes to know how they would have gleamed with the comment. And that little detail alone was enough to infuriate her. She shouldn't know him so well. *But she did.*

And it pissed her off almost more than the fact that he was in her bathroom uninvited.

"Get out!" she hissed.

"No can do, Faith."

"What?" She was going to start throwing shampoo bottles at him if he didn't get his ass out of her bathroom and soon. "Of course you can."

"Well, sure. I can…but I'm moving in, so I need to—"

"You are *what?*"

Logan was a lot of things. Primarily he was way too cocky for his own good, way too sexy for *her* own good and besides both of those things, an almost constant, annoying presence in her life. Like a pebble in her shoe. Yes, he was a lot of things. But an idiot wasn't one of them. So why would he think he was—

"Oh no," she said as soon as she connected the dots in her head. "You are *not* moving in."

"I have to," he said simply. "You're the love of my life, remember?"

#

Logan Langdon was very aware that he was pushing it. A lot. He was also very aware that he was enjoying every moment of it. Faith Turner was sexy, sassy and whether she would ever admit it or not, completely into him.

But damn, he certainly hoped she'd admit it and soon. Because as much fun as it was to pursue her, he was positively certain that it would be even more fun to *catch* her.

"You are not the love of my life, Logan." Faith's voice was

starting to reach an impressively high frequency. "Get. Out. Of. My. *Bathroom!*"

Leaving her alone was probably for the best, after all, she *was* in the shower. It hadn't been his intention to interrupt her privacy, but he couldn't lie, now that he too was in the bathroom with her naked wet body only a few feet away, it was the last place he wanted to leave.

Still.

Logan grabbed a large towel off a nearby hook and draped it over the edge of the glass. "Here. Cover up if you must. But I'm not leaving. I'm moving in." He grinned even though he knew she wouldn't see it, turned and left the bathroom to wait for her in the adjoining bedroom.

Logan didn't miss the growl of frustration she let out as he left the room, nor did he miss the tightening in his belly at the sound. There was something about riling her up that he enjoyed. Maybe a little too much.

He didn't have to wait long for a dripping wet, steaming mad, Faith wrapped in only the towel he'd provided her, to join him.

Fuck. Should have given her a smaller towel.

The image made his lips curl up into a grin.

"What are you smiling at?" she demanded. "And what the hell are you doing here?"

Even if he hadn't put the picture of Faith in a much smaller towel in his head, Logan would have been distracted. After all, the most gorgeous woman he knew, with all of her perfectly proportioned curves was currently standing directly in front of him, the soft mounds of her breasts pushing up from where she'd cinched the towel around her, the opening of said towel displaying just enough thigh for him to fixate on, with her long blond hair hanging wet over her shoulders giving an air of some watery fantasy vibes that more than anything, Logan desperately wanted to explore.

He swallowed hard and hoped his arousal wasn't betraying him too obviously because it was taking all the self control he had not to pull her in for a kiss to show her exactly what it was that she did to him. If that last kiss they'd shared was any indication, he was sure that those feelings weren't completely one sided. Not that she was going to admit it.

Not yet anyway.

"Logan! Are you even listening to me?"

Yanked from his fantasies of what was under the towel, Logan refocused on the issue at hand. He was moving in and she was clearly not happy about it.

He swallowed hard and turned to the dresser, pulling open a drawer. "I was just wondering which drawers I could make mine." He grinned as he reached inside and pulled out a silky pair of light pink panties. "Pink, huh? I didn't take you for a baby pink kind of woman." He dangled the panties in front of him. "Red? Definitely. Black? Absolutely. But soft pink?" he pressed his lips together in an effort not to smirk. "Now that is a surprise."

Faith's face had also turned a specific shade of pink, but there was nothing soft about it when she reached out and yanked her panties from his grip before reaching past him and shutting the drawer shut so violently he almost got his hand caught inside.

"Get. Out. Logan."

Okay. He was definitely pushing her too far.

He let his eyes drop to where her towel had slipped a little and for a split second contemplated again how it might turn out if he just gave in and kissed her, but the anger flashing in her eyes told him it wouldn't be a good idea.

"Okay," he finally conceded. "I'll let you get dressed and then we can talk." He watched her visibly—at least a little—relax as he spoke. "Because we do need to talk about this, Faith and you know it." She nodded but she still didn't look pleased.

"Don't forget, you're the love of my life." Her lips pressed together in a hard line when he added, "At least for the next few weeks."

Fighting Happily Ever After*, **Faith and Logan's story is next!

Don't forget to join my mailing list where you'll be the first to hear about new stories, sales and promotions and giveaways!
You can join me here —>
https://elenaaitken.com/newsletter/

About the Author

Elena Aitken is a USA Today Bestselling Author of more than forty romance and women's fiction novels. Living a stone's throw from the Rocky Mountains with her teenager twins, their two cats and a goofy rescue dog, Elena escapes into the mountains whenever life allows. She can often be found with her toes in the lake and a glass of wine in her hand, dreaming up her next book and working on her own happily ever after with her very own mountain man.

To learn more about Elena:
www.elenaaitken.com
elena@elenaaitken.com